Peter Sale was born in Liverpool and received his education at Saint Joseph's Academy of Hard Knocks. He left school at fourteen, ready for adventure, and, after ducking bombs with the American Red Cross in London, chasing Nazis in Hamburg, training with the New Zealand Air Force, writing country music in Nashville and appearing in Hollywood TV commercials, he settled down to write about his childhood memories in *Tom Kipper's Schooldays*. Peter now lives with his wife Carmelisa in a town called Paradise, California, where he is at work on his second Tom Kipper novel.

Tom Kipper's Schooldays was originally published in the USA under the title *A River of Scouse*.

Tom Kipper's Schooldays

Memories of an Irish Childhood in Liverpool

Peter Sale

First published in Great Britain in 2007
by HEADLINE PUBLISHING GROUP

First published in paperback in 2007
by HEADLINE PUBLISHING GROUP

1

Cataloguing in Publication Data is available from the British Library

ISBN 978 0 7553 3677 7

Typeset in Sabon by Avon DataSet Ltd,
Bidford-on-Avon, Warwickshire

Printed and bound in Great Britain by
Mackays of Chatham plc, Chatham, Kent

Headline's policy is to use papers that are natural, renewable and
recyclable products and made from wood grown in sustainable forests. The
logging and manufacturing processes are expected to conform to the
environmental regulations of the country of origin.

HEADLINE PUBLISHING GROUP
A division of Hachette Livre UK Ltd
338 Euston Road
London NW1 3BH

www.headline.co.uk
www.hodderheadline.com

To Carmelisa Azuara Sale.
The Mexican Scouser
Who wishes to remain anonymous.

Prologue

♣

When they came to Ireland, it was never a cordial visit.
They came often. Saxons, Jutes, Angles, Picts, and
barbarians swarmed across the Irish countryside to loot,
burn, and pillage – never once with a twinkle in their eye.

Why did they bother? Why did they not just leave the
poor old Celts in their rock caves with their goats and
sheep and shamrock?

Then came the Normans to civilise, to bring order out
of chaos – not a smart thing to do with the Irish, who
abhor bureaucracy. Lastly arrived the English with pomp
and circumstance and a new language, which so annoyed
the jolly old Irish that they took the jolly old English
language and added spice, charm, or a turn of phrase; to
whittle it, turn it upside down, and thread its fabric with
colour and vibrancy. And when they were finished,
English-English was a clodhopper – a plodding, feeble

communication without a soul. Irish-English was in!

When all of the invasions had ceased of this farthest western outpost of Europe, the potato blight struck in the middle of the nineteenth century and the exodus began. The shores that had once teemed with savage invaders now teemed with migrants boarding ketch, steamer, or schooner, outward bound to Australia, Britain, Canada, and America. With them they took their Irish-English, their hunger, their laughter, and their thirst.

After invading Liverpool, they moved 'across the water' – a euphemism for crossing the River Mersey – to the County of Cheshire, where at Birkenhead they built the mightiest ships in the world to cross the Atlantic.

But it was way past famine time, so they never took these ships themselves but stayed instead to become the 'Liverpool Irish' and make Liverpool in England the capital of Ireland. In their cups, swimming in Merseyside nostalgia, they will sing:

> 'Coz I got the Liverpool Blues
> And when I die
> Don't bury me at all
> Just hang my bones
> In Saint George's Hall . . .

And they invented 'scouse', a dish reminiscent of Irish stew but with leeks from the Welsh and order from the Lancastrians. It rises above kippers and marmalade as the Liverpool dish so that people from Liverpool, those

Liverpool Irish, became known as 'Scousers'.

The Scouse language held the tribe together like good glue, a fractured syntax, with meanings beyond the comprehension of lower mortals. It was a River of Scouse.

Thus it was that we historical Kippers (the family, not the smelly herring), living close to but not actually in Liverpool, were regarded by Scousers as colonials beyond the pale of genuine Scouseland, for we lived 'across the water' in the County of Cheshire, famous for its cats and cheese. But I still maintain:

I am a Scouser
My name is Tom Kipper
And this is my story
Or at least the beginning . . .

Chapter One

Bart Finnegan

Bart Finnegan was my uncle.

He was short in stature and long on refunds to his creditors, who were legion. But he had a great heart. Anything he had was yours. And vice versa.

He was a very sharp and wiry man, as Irish a face as ever graced the pubs of Dublin, wry of humour, perpetual of thirst. Canon O'Malley of Saint Joseph's had a soft spot for Uncle Bart, even though he knew of his adventurous spirit in back street economy, and would warm to conversation whenever they met, which was usually on the steps of the church after Mass on a Sunday.

'Kippers,' he expounded to Bart, in the thin rays of winter sunshine on the church steps, 'are my favourite meal of the day.'

'With marmalade,' said Bart.

'Aye, with marmalade. Good day to you, Mrs

Shaunnassey and Mr Shaunnassey. The best ones are from Grimsby.'

'I'll keep that in mind, Father,' said Bart.

Uncle Bart joined us on Tuesday with my mother, Mary Catherine, his sister, as we went to O'Connell Street market for the weekly provisions; the baby, my sister Elizabeth, in the perambulator; and I hanging on the side in case I walked into a bus as Quentin Kipper did. I was ten years old, absorbing everything I could in the magic world where grownups said and did strange things, like drinking beer and smoking cigarettes.

Halfway down O'Connell Street on the right-hand side, across the street from Lloyd's Chemist, was Reilly's Fish, a trestled cavern of aromatic vapours. As red-headed an Irishman as ever sold haddock, Reilly smelled and gawped like a large cod himself, with a straw hat anchoring his red thatch and a blue-and-white apron tied across his rotund girth, a blessing from Guinness.

On the wall that wasn't window or door hung his fireman's shield with his name engraved in the brass, Sean Reilly, County Fireman, Ten Year Veteran. It was embossed with the county seal. A picture of Fireman Reilly and the fire team standing in front of the big red engine with ladders hung next to the big brass shield.

'What can I be doing for you now, Mary?' he asked.

'I see you've still got the picture up, Sean,' answered my mother, looking for a bargain. It was whispered that Reilly would set fire to his own house if he could put it out.

'Aye, Mary, as fine a team of lads as ever quenched a fire!'

'And a thirst,' said Bart.

My ten-year-old brain was absorbing the ritual of buying fish when I noticed Uncle Aloysius Finnegan, Bart and my mother's brother, outside Lloyd's Chemists, smoking a cigarette, loitering by the side of a County Rubbish container full of litter. I didn't remember having seen Uncle Al smoking cigarettes before.

'Do you have any cod?' asked my mother.

'The very finest, freshest cod from out of the depths of the Atlantic Ocean.'

'Really! Last time it smelled as if it were from Guinness Brewery.'

'Ah, Mary, now!'

I clung to the handle of the perambulator, or pram, for such was it called, admiring the great interchange of intelligence in the commerce of fish, with the baby Elizabeth lying in the accommodating circumference of this mid-Victorian vehicle with the false bottom. The pram I mean, not the child.

There is a word that will set in motion all the exuberance and fright that can be possibly mustered, summoned by any human being. The word will make his pulses pound and the very heart jump within him. That word is FIRE! And if there is one man in the Irish universe whose blood boils within his Gaelic veins at this delightful cry, it is Sean Reilly, the ten-year fireman.

When it came from across O'Connell Street from

outside of Lloyd's Chemist, flames leaping great fingers from the garbage pail, Fireman Reilly reached for the fine red fire extinguisher on the wall by his brass plaque and leaped like a scalded Kerry cat across O'Connell Street.

Which was when Uncle Bartholomew Finnegan slipped with easy grace into Reilly's Fish, picked up a case of fine Grimsby kippers, and said to me, 'Pick up the baby!'

If it were not for the urgency of his command, I would have enquired why, but with a deftness beyond my understanding, I picked up Elizabeth, and Bart slipped the case of kippers with consummate care into the hold at the bottom of the carriage.

'Put the baby back,' said he, which I did with further alacrity. I was being introduced into the commerce of fish by a senior executive.

'We are going,' said Uncle Bart to my mother, 'for a wee walk, Mary. Finish your shopping.'

At a smooth pace, we manoeuvred the perambulator the length of O'Connell Street, taking a left at Doyle's Corner, down Rake Lane, through the tradesmen's entrance at Saint Joseph's School, which cut short to the door of the rectory.

It was Flora O'Toole who answered the door with the polished brass doorknob and the gleaming knocker. She was as old as the school itself, as old as the church, as old as the canon. She had always been there; the gargoyles knew her, young priests feared her, the altar boys kept their distance, and the grimy old pigeons flew away startled. But she allowed a faint glimmer of a smile to show on that taut mouth when she saw Uncle Bart, for Bart had style. Everybody loved Bart. He was born with glitter.

'Bartholomew Finnegan, what can I do for you, Bart?' The Adam's apple jigged up and down under a Victorian brooch that held the black crepe tight to her scrawny neck.

'Ah, Miss O'Toole,' said Bart, 'some of the men from the Saint Vincent de Paul Society and I decided to give the canon a small token of our esteem for all that he has done for us over the blessed year.'

I lifted up the baby while Bart took out the crate of aromatic Grimsby kippers. 'This is it, Miss O'Toole.'

'Why, Bartholomew, how considerate of you. Please call me Flora.'

'Aye, now, it's nothing. There is just one consideration: we would like the gift to be anonymous. Please don't let the canon know who brought it to his doorstep.'

Bart took the box inside, and when he returned smiling, he had twenty shillings in his hand and his step was light. The following Sunday, after the nine o'clock Mass was over, Uncle Bart was coming down the steps of the church at the same time as I was when Canon O'Malley summoned him back inside.

'Bart,' said he, 'a very fine anonymous donor has given me a crate of delicious Grimsby kippers. They're splendid. If you go around to see Flora, she'll give you a brace.' And when Bart came home with me, he gave the kippers to my mother, who made him a cup of tea.

'We made twenty shillings, Mary,' he said, 'nine to you for the use of the pram, one to Tom who lifted the baby and will never say a word of this to anyone, and five to me.'

Pouring the tea, my mother said, 'That comes to fifteen by my reckoning.'

'Oh, yes, five to my fine brother, Aloysius, who I'm just about to meet.'

'And how does Aloysius figure into your chicanery?'

'Aloysius? Oh, he's the one who started the fire.'

Before Uncle Bart headed off in the direction of that hospitable inn of dubious reputation, the Bird in Hand, my mother said to him at the door, 'The canon gave me a message for you.'

'And what would that be, Mary?'

'He said that will be five Our Fathers and five Hail Marys.'

Chapter Two

Marx

♣

Right in the middle of his active career of doing nothing, my father found Karl Marx. Or Marx found him. The finding unveiled a revelation that he had been inwardly searching for most of his life, for within the Marxian dogma he found a genuine morally uplifting, conscience-cleansing reason for doing nothing.

'The Capitalist system,' said my father, 'floats on the backs of the workers. Without the cheap labour the Capitalist employer uses to prop up his empire, he would be instantly bankrupt. The law, which is an ass, accommodates this corrupt betrayal of the worker. The answer, Karl Marx said, is not to work!'

I looked in awe at him, for I had heard people say he was a genius. My mother said he was a genius only at not working. He called himself a 'ragged trousered philanthropist', expounding his philosophy wherever he found a willing audience.

Of course we had nothing to eat, the table was bare, and we were two and a half years behind in the rent. 'This Karl Marx,' offered my mother, 'do you think he could find you a job?'

'That's the point, woman,' my father, Joseph Prendergast Kipper, philosopher, fumed. 'Under the Communist Manifesto, you don't work; thus you defeat the Capitalist system. It's that simple!' He started to roll himself a cigarette from a canister of strange, black tobacco.

My mother ladled mashed potatoes from the pan to the plate, smacking the big spoon on the side of the pan. 'I'm not talking about the Capitalists,' she said. 'You've found a good excuse not to work for the Capitalists, courtesy of your comrade in Moscow. But why not work for this Mr Marx instead?'

'Karl Marx,' fumed my father, spilling over at this woman who talked so much nonsense, 'lives in Russia.'

My mother smacked the ladle against the big potato pan. 'He's a foreigner then,' she said. 'He's not English or even Irish for that matter, and he's telling you how to run your country.'

'I am neither an Athenian nor a Greek but a citizen of the world,' triumphed Joseph Prendergast, spitting out shards of black tobacco.

Mother put a plate of mashed potatoes in front of him. 'Will it be the Athenian or the Greek,' she asked, 'who will be down at the Labour Exchange tomorrow looking for a handout, while all his children and his poor suffering wife eat mashed potatoes every day and not much else?'

'Don't worry, woman, we shall overcome. There'll be a new day!'

The only new day I knew of was the next day when I set off as usual for the Catholic elementary school, Saint Joseph's Academy of Hard Knocks we called it, the year before the war began.

The previous years were five blissful pre-McCann years with Saint Joseph's Sisters praying us through innocent childhood kicking each other's shins. But now I was a pupil at the big school and on the new day in question I nearly lost my ear. Miss McCann was an ear-puller, and while she pulled she twisted her mouth to one side of her skinny face. But we had a respite that day, or so I thought, for just as soon as the assembly bell rang, our pale, anaemic English bodies with mostly Irish names were marched off to church, which was next door. This piece of luck happened only on days of Holy Obligation, which meant that it was a holiday. I whooped for sheer joy. It was a day of freedom from ear-puller McCann, Dracula.

I was out through the church gates like one of Uncle Bart's whippets just as soon as we received the final blessing, racing down Primrose Lane with music in my heart, back to home, where my mother said, 'What on earth are you doing here? Why aren't you at school?'

'It's a holiday. It's a feast day – a Holy Day of Obligation.'

'It's nothing of the sort,' said my mother, wiping her hands on her apron.

'Yes, it is, Ma. I think it's Saint Patrick's Day.'

'Saint Patrick's Day is March seventeenth,' she answered, 'which was last month, so off you go back to school.'

'There could be two Saint Patrick's days,' I ventured.

'And two Saint Patricks?'

My minuscule heart sank. I could not comprehend the idea of going back to Miss McCann's penitentiary to have my ears further lengthened without benefit of anaesthetic. My glorious day of kicking cans and chasing cats down the alley was disappearing like so much chaff in the wind. 'But Ma, we went to Mass!'

'And good for your soul it was, too! Off you go!'

I didn't move. My bag of skin and bones remained resolute. The time had arrived to take a stand for freedom. 'Dad said Karl Marx said not to go to work, so why should I go to school?'

This was followed by a smack across the ear.

I wept bitterly at my defeat by the Capitalist system as I crawled back up Primrose Lane to Saint Joseph's Academy of Hard Knocks.

The kid who blocked my shuffling gait was bigger than I was with a cap on his fat head from the grammar school down at the Cross. His school and mine had been at war since Henry the Eighth sacked the monasteries. Tufts of red hair stuck out from his cap like wheat in a barn. He smiled like a big fat executioner. 'You hit my little brother last week,' he commenced, preparing his case for the guillotine and my neck.

'No, I didn't. Honest,' I cried.

'Yes, you did. I remember your rotten face.'

My move to dodge his revenge for his fallen brother was to no avail, for he caught me in mid-stride with a thump of his pudgy fist in my left ear that sent me sprawling against the locked doors of the Bird in Hand, a seedy tavern of mediocre repute. When I picked up my bones, Fat Boy was whistling down the lane and I crawled to Saint Joseph's Academy of Hard Knocks.

By this time, my left ear had received two assaults on its person, one loving clump by my mother to drive home Christian values and one by Fat Boy to drive them out again. When Miss McCann saw my fearful and distressed state as I fell through her doorway, the whole classroom of Catholic boys and girls turned the assault of their combined gaze upon me.

'What have we here?' enquired Spiderlady McCann, placing her glasses upon her lumpy, bony nose. 'What do you think about this, class?' she asked with twisted mouth.

All my former friends and allies, Mickey O'Brien, Jimmy O'Connell, and Charlie Murphy, all twisted their mouths like Spiderlady McCann. Suddenly they didn't know me. I was sinking and they were pushing me under.

'Isn't he horrible?' she asked.

'Horrible,' they all agreed.

'Awful!'

'Oh, yes, most awful!'

'Didn't even comb his hair this morning.'

'I didn't have a comb,' I said.

'No comb! Ha, ha, ha, ha. What do you think of that, class?'

'Ha, ha, ha, ha.'

She took me by the left ear, which was now the size of an army blanket, and pulled me towards her in a twisting motion so that my face and hers were two inches apart at most. I could see the bony protrusions of her gaunt cheeks, the rivers of blue veins pulsing in her forehead; she was a dragonlady with fetid breath and teeth like the Pennine Chain. Her most feared weapon, the carpenter's pencil, began to rap my knuckles with tortuous rhythm.

'Late for class,' she said. 'Didn't even comb your hair. Tom Kipper, you are a disgrace to Saint Joseph's!'

There comes a time in every boy's life when he exults in his freedom, throwing aside the yoke of the Barbarians. The push I gave had her tripping backward over the dais on which her desk sat. The class rose in awe at David and Goliath. She screamed at Billy McGovern and Dan Considine to hold me over the desk as she picked up her swishing cane. Billy McGovern was easy. I punched him straight in the gut and he fell over a chair, while I gave Dan Considine the beady eye and he just got out of my way.

I didn't even close the door as I stepped out into the freedom of the playground, the empty playground, with the church steeple in the background, the sun in the sky, the trees green with spring. I will never go back to school again, I said. And I never did. Well, my body did. But not my heart.

'Dad,' I asked later in the evening over a plate of mashed potatoes, 'will Karl Marx kill all teachers?'

'Just some of them,' answered my father.

Chapter Three

The Second Collection

Despite her name, Miss Hanratty was not Irish. Not Irish like my mother was, anyway, or Auntie Madge or Auntie Moira. She practised a very precise, polished, unimaginative English accent that made her purse her lips and open her mouth like a gawping goldfish so that the words were forced out like soap bubbles. And she told us how badly we all spoke except for a cluster of favourite girls who occupied benches at the circumference of her raised desk and would chorus, 'Yes, Miss Hanratty,' whenever she opened her goldfish mouth. Her dominion extended, of course, to us Irish kids, who sought sanctuary in the back rows, in the grime instead of the glitter, forever watching a clock that never moved. We were like the bounds of the British Empire she was always rattling on about, which, whenever they appalled Whitehall with vague ideas of freedom, were sent a gunboat instead of an ambassador.

Miss Hanratty's gunboat was a carpenter's rule with which she rattled our knuckles until they resembled choice bananas with blue stickers. That is, until the arrival of Molly Maguire, Mrs Molly Maguire. Her husband, Cooley Maguire, was the town bookie. He was legitimate and not legitimate; he was licensed and unlicensed. He was a most sharp dresser was Cooley Maguire, very sharp indeed for his common upbringing, unschooled, soft of speech, buoyant, diplomatic, and shifty, obeying all the nuances of the law, which my father called an ass. As night fell, so did Cooley Maguire's observance of the books of statute. No bookie ever took more illegal bets than Mr Maguire did.

Molly Maguire, Cooley's missus, was a great fluttering hen of a woman, well preserved, dressed like a peacock, and wearing bright, shining, crimson lipstick. She supported Cooley like a great mother hen, so her husband would know that when he returned from horses and hounds, Guinness and pickled ham sandwiches were waiting. She was bigger and broader than Cooley was, but he was the boss. Well, he thought so.

Joey Maguire lounged at the back of Miss Hanratty's class in the company of his peers, always better dressed, no less a ruffian. 'I'm going to tell my mother about you,' he sobbed as the carpenter's rule fell mercilessly upon his knuckles. 'Just you wait!'

It was a most splendid day when Joey Maguire's mother arrived, for she gave no warning of her historic visit. Bypassing the convention of making an appointment with the headmaster, she just marched through the chalk dust of Saint Joseph's Academy of Hard Knocks, past the corridor's leaky heaters, and opened the door to the classroom. She then caught the bird-like eye of Miss Hanratty and hooked a forefinger to indicate the direction in which she should travel – which was the corridor – and Hanratty moved, mesmerised, in that direction. Nobody ever interrupted class. Regulations in giant tomes told faculty and student immemorial that class should never be interrupted. Even the headmaster would knock discreetly should he ever even think of entering. But the moving finger of Molly Maguire worked the oracle. When Miss Hanratty moved through the doorway and into the corridor, leaving the door partly open, forty of us kids stared, slack-jawed and open-eyed, at the two figures silhouetted behind the frosted glass.

Then began the torrent, the river of words gushing from the brassy throat of Molly Maguire. We did not hear the entire torrent, for Miss Hanratty was trying to close the door, which kept springing open enough for us to hear. 'You bloody bitch . . . you ever hit my Joey again . . . spread you all over . . . I don't give a . . . lay a hand on him and . . . mincemeat . . . marmalade . . . shitty . . .' We just loved the words. We all looked at Joey as the figures danced and pirouetted on the other side of the glass. Joey was smiling with one of his feet on the desk. Hey, he had given due warning – we Maguires stick together. All of us Irish kids were jumping for joy. Nobody had ever, ever spoken like that to Hanratty; she was der Führer of the faculty. Even the janitors avoided her. The 'chosen few' girls in the Royal Circle up front of the class were shuddering and faking a good weep. The door slammed. Steps in the corridor went this way and then steps in the corridor went that way.

It was then that we all started talking at once until the headmaster arrived with the news that we would be splitting up for the rest of the day into various classes as Miss Hanratty had a severe headache. We whooped for sheer joy.

In the schoolyard, Sullivan said to Joey Maguire, 'Is your dad a bookie?'

'I don't know,' said Joey. 'Ask my ma.' This gave full import to the hierarchy of the Maguire clan. It was an absolutely grand day.

'Tell me what happened again,' said my mother, peeling big potatoes with the skill of a surgeon.

Billy Payne was oddly mannered, saying please and thank you and never, ever getting involved in a fight, which was an unthinkable way of living. Getting into a 'scrap' in the schoolyard was therapeutic, banishing inhibitions and loosing hostility. It was most necessary to us Irish kids. What was life without a good smack in the kisser? Giving, not receiving. So we called him a 'sissy', reciting, 'Billy Payne lost his brain.'

'Do unto others as you would have others do unto you,' said Billy Payne. 'And my name is William, not Billy!'

'That's what Hanratty says,' sneered Sullivan.

'It's from the Bible,' said Billy.

'Then why does she hit us?' jibed back Sullivan.

Billy Payne had no answer to this, so Sullivan said, 'Sissy!' and shoved him against the school wall.

But Billy's attitude bothered us. How could we go through life not hitting each other? It caught me in its moral net. No matter how you jeered at him, he wouldn't fight back. That spelled disaster for the human race. Huns and Visigoths and Picts just had to slaughter each other; otherwise, there'd be no history.

Hanratty didn't return to the Academy of Hard Knocks until Monday, when she drove in her tiny Vauxhall to her minuscule parking spot under the oak growing over the rusty brick wall from the church garden. Nobody was allowed within many yards of that slate grey Vauxhall.

Joey Maguire was assigned a solitary bench at the rear of the classroom where he was isolated in great majesty, firing off rubber bands, eating sweets, breaking pencil points, and spilling ink, with no text or exercise books. Henrietta Hanratty said nothing but snorted audibly, seething at this thorn in her self-esteem.

As the school clock struck ten, Mrs Molly Maguire opened the door, smiled at Joey, said 'Good morning' to Hanratty, closed the door, and clacked away. Henrietta Hanratty ground her teeth in frustration. Joey read a comic book.

* * *

Mr Quentin Sullivan was a window washer who sometimes helped keep the bar at the Dirty Duck. The Sullivans lived down a crooked little street not far from the school called Saint James Lane, which was a more than adequate name as it had neither grace nor style, even though it had the blessing of that saint. It seemed inhabited by gangs of Sullivans, all the kids with freckles, beige skin, large teeth, and red hair glued in patches to their Irish heads. They filled a large portion of the church at the nine o'clock Mass, at which Canon Maginnity was the usual celebrant.

The second collection seemed always for schools, bringing in sixpences, perhaps, sometimes just pennies, while the main collection showed receipt of silver shillings, half-crowns, ten-shilling notes, and sometimes even a seemingly large pound note.

'The collectors brought in their monies,' said Uncle Bart, 'and they were all transferred to one canvas bag for the bank. Then it disappeared.'

'Just vanished?' asked my mother, Mary Catherine Kipper, pouring tea.

'Just vanished,' confirmed Bart.

'How much?'

'About thirty-five pounds, probably.'

'You didn't take it for the ponies, did you, Bart?' asked Aunt Madge. They all laughed and sipped their tea.

Bart said, 'The canon questioned everybody.'

'Were the police notified?' asked Aunt Moira, nibbling an Eccles cake.

'Nah,' said Bart. 'The canon probably thinks whoever pulled it off will bring it to the confessional box sometime and he'll charge them interest.'

They all laughed again.

'Wasn't Quentin Sullivan one of the collectors?' my mother asked.

'Aye,' said Bart. 'He and Jimmy Phelan, me and Pat Donohue.'

'Did you split it between the four of you?' queried Aunt Madge.

I went out to County Park, thinking about the utterly enormous amount of thirty-five pounds stolen from the church in broad daylight. If it had been from the Bank of England, I would have cheered because they can just print more. But from the church – boy, that must be a mortal sin, almost anyway.

With his battered cricket bat, Sullivan sliced at the equally battered tennis ball to send it soaring over the tall sandstone wall between the playground and the church garden. 'That's a six,' said Sullivan, showing an expansive row of teeth and gums.

'And you have to get the ball,' said Jimmy Reilly.

Placing just one foot in the church garden was trespassing, punishable with six of 'the stick' from Headmaster 'Pop' Devereaux, whose right arm was as dextrous as Sullivan's when delivering sixes.

Miss Henrietta Hanratty's slug grey Vauxhall sedan lay parked in isolation, bumper against the sandstone wall.

'Is Horrible Hanny about?' asked Sullivan, surveying the yard.

'All clear,' said Jimmy Reilly.

Sullivan clunked up on the bonnet of Miss Hanratty's Vauxhall with haste born of fear, and he shimmied up and over the sandstone wall, which we leaned against awaiting his return, looking as guileless as two axe murderers.

'Hello, Tom Kipper,' said Moira McGuinness – 'Spotty Face' we called her.

'Go away,' I said.

'What are you doing?'

'She's deaf,' said Jimmy Reilly.

'You're doing something,' said Moira McGuinness.

'We're saying our morning prayers,' I said.

'It's past twelve o'clock. How can you be saying your morning prayers?'

'We forgot,' said Reilly, 'like you forgot your mind!'

'You're nasty!' she stamped. 'How can you call yourselves Catholics?'

'Has she gone?' whispered Sullivan from over the wall.

'Yes, come on!' We walked some steps away from the wall.

'What's keeping him?' asked Jimmy Reilly.

'He's over,' I said, 'but I think he's under Hanny's car.'

Sullivan ran out with the ball, but before we had the opportunity to commence another inning, Mrs Irene O'Toole rang her big brass bell and we slouched back to Hanratty's penitentiary.

'See me after class,' hissed Sullivan.

'What's up?' I asked.

'Tell you later.'

As we filed into the corridor, Joey Maguire tripped up Billy Payne and said, 'Sorry, Billy,' with a most splendid sneer.

'Now, class,' pouted Miss Hanratty, 'we shall mark our chart for Daily Mass. Put your hands up, those who went to Mass and Holy Communion this morning.'

She displayed a chart on the wall behind her, full of silver stars, each of which represented an attendance against a student's name. I put my hand up with about six other kids, including Joey Maguire. Miss Hanratty placed stars on the chart but looked at me and then at Joey Maguire with those pursed lips and a sniff as though she were harbouring dubious thoughts. Joey Maguire sported more stars than anybody else did. Every day he put his hand up. And every day I knew he never went to Mass. So did Hanratty. But Joey's stars glittered. Perhaps he gambled like his dad, Cooley.

'Hey, Sully,' I said as we ran into the yard after school was over, 'how come you didn't put your hand up for Mass? I saw you there.'

'Because I don't want her shitty stars,' said Sullivan.

From that day on I joined the no-hands-up brigade, and my stars fell from Hanratty's heavenly chart.

'Over here,' said Sullivan. He looked right and left, then leaned under Hanratty's Vauxhall, picked up a bag of sorts, put it under his shirt, and hurried to the gate. 'Come on.'

'Where are we going?'

'To County Park.'

'What for?'

'I've got something to show you.'

The park was close by, early daffodils springing eagerly in boisterous profusion, almost laughing with joy, blossoms on some zestful trees, the massive oaks, some said one hundred years old, some two hundred, feet firmly placed in English soil holding all together. The cricket ground was deserted and the Pavilion in duck white just sat there, looking as if it held amiable secrets. We sat on the steps to the back entrance as Sullivan pulled the canvas bag from under his grubby beige shirt.

'Look,' he said, turning it upside down.

Out spilled silver sixpences, shillings, florins, half-crowns, ten-shilling notes, and even three big one-pound notes.

'Whoopee!' cried Sullivan.

'Saint Joseph be praised,' I said, borrowing from my mother. 'Where did you get it?'

'In the church garden under a bush.'

I'd never seen such money, such profusion. 'How much is it?'

'I don't know. Let's count it. How many shillings in a pound?'

'Twenty.'

There were over thirty-nine pounds. Sully and I ran our fingers through it. It felt like power. 'What are we going to do with it?' I asked.

'It's mine,' said Sullivan. 'I'm going to give it to me ma.'

'Your ma?'

'Yes. She needs a new dress and shoes.'

'It's stolen,' I said.

'Stolen?'

'It's the collection money stolen last Sunday.'

'Nah,' said Sullivan. 'Somebody robbed a bank.'

'It's got Saint Joseph's on the bag.' We sat on the Pavilion steps looking at each other until it started to drizzle. 'Your ma will know.'

'Then we'll buy brand-new cricket bats and a football.'

'Banana splits,' I suggested.

'A packet of Woodbines and matches.'

'What about a cigarette lighter?'

'New footer boots.'

'Chocolate milk shakes.'

'A fishing line. Two fishing lines.'

'Let's hide it.'

Sully found a small space through which he could squeeze his skinny Irish body under the Pavilion, crawling to the middle and crawling back again smeared in red mud. 'I put it on top of a beam,' he wheezed.

By the time I got home, the April gloom was coming in. My mother said, 'Where on earth have you been?'

'Playing cops and robbers with Paddy Sullivan.'

'Were you a cop or a robber?'

'I robbed a bank, Ma,' I said.

The arms of Morpheus took me in instant embrace as

I pulled the covers that night and I was wading through knee-high bank notes and silver with more raining from heaven. I bought a big golden spaniel named Rex to pull me along on sparkling new roller skates, eating toffee apples and liquorice sticks stored in my tree house with a grand skull-and-crossbones flying from its mast.

Sully and I had Hanratty tied to a stake. She was begging for ice cream to slake her thirst as we slurped large gobs. Still the money fell.

It was a grand secret we took to school the next day, enjoying the balm our nouveau riche heritage had brought.

'It's like *Great Expectations*,' I said to Sully.

'It's like owning your own bank,' he replied.

'Today,' said Hanratty, 'we will study the Ten Commandments and how they affect our lives. Open your catechisms at page twenty-three. Tom Kipper can start reading, for we should fear God and keep his commandments!' She didn't ask Joey Maguire to read. Kevin O'Leary read the second and third commandments. Snotty Noreen Gallagher read four, five, and six. Hanratty read with great drama the seventh, 'Thou shalt not steal,' quivering her voice, rolling her pink eyeballs, and banging her stick.

'Do you know what, students? Last Sunday a thief stole the nine o'clock collection, money that belongs to God. With sinister deceit this man purloined Our Lord's treasury.'

'It could have been a woman,' said Joey Maguire,

firing off a rubber band, 'or a girl.' All the prim and proper girls in the Royal Circle turned to hiss at him.

The interruption upset Miss Hanratty; only men would do such foul deeds. 'What utter darkness must lie in his heart,' she simpered.

'Or her heart,' said Joey Maguire.

The hairs stood to attention on my head, goose bumps all over my scalp. In the play yard I said, 'We gotta give it back.'

'I know,' said Sully.

Just before school started the following day, we went to see 'Pop' Devereaux. 'Please, sir,' we said, almost together, 'we found this under a bush in the church garden.'

'Pop' Devereaux's eyes bugged out. 'Well, boys, now let me see, you're Francis Sullivan and you're Thomas Kipper, from Miss Hanratty's class, hmm?'

'Yes, sir.'

'When did you find this?'

'This morning, sir,' we lied.

'Well, now, boys, there just might be a reward for this.' We received a shilling each for our honesty, at which accolade we bowed our heads, not for modesty, which was assumed, but for shame. Well, not too much.

'What did you do with your shilling?' I asked Sully in our secret place at the Pavilion.

'I gave it to me ma. What did you do with yours?'

'I gave it to me ma, too, but she gave me a sixpence back.'

'What about some ice cream?'

Over a big chocolate chip at Wall's, Sully said, 'I don't understand me dad. He told me ma that he was going to buy her a dress and some shoes, but the next day he was as mad as a hatter, said someone stole his money. And me dad hasn't worked for years, just like yours. So Ma gave him the shilling and sent him to the Bird in Hand for beer. Said she felt sorry for him.'

'Saint Joseph be praised,' I said, borrowing from my mother again. 'Want another chocolate chip?'

'Yeah!'

Chapter Four

Schwenk

♣

'Vy do all you English boys have Irish names?' queried Mr Schwenk, eyes swimming through the thick lenses like goldfish in a bowl.

Nobody answered. We stood behind our workbenches waiting for him to start woodwork class, while he swished a cane gently. 'Eh? Nobody has an answer? Irish names in England?' A moth was trapped behind the windowpane. Mr Schwenk moved gently towards it, swishing the cane.

'Germans kill without mercy,' whispered Sullivan in my ear. 'Me dad told me.'

Schwenk raised the cane. All red and scruffy Irish heads turned. He pushed the window gently open. The moth fluttered through and away into the weak northern light, which glimmered for a moment in Mr Schwenk's eyes. 'Now boys,' he raised his voice, 'today ve shall all learn how to use a plane. To plane correctly. Vith precision. Ve shall all do a good job. Now come up here and vatch as I plane this piece of vood, doing all things right.'

'Maybe he's not a German,' I whispered to Sullivan.

'He's a Hun,' said Sullivan. 'Me dad told me.'

We watched the sawdust-covered clock for break time when Schwenk wasn't looking, for if he caught us, he became irritated that we should consider his class boring, smacking his bench with a cane and uttering words our frail Irish minds could not comprehend but found fascinating. This day, before recess, he had us tidy our workspaces and said, 'Boys, von of you has stolen a drill; not a very modern piece of equipment, but von vich I must pay for if it is not returned. It vas taken last veek ven you vere here last. Bring it back next veek, and no more vill be said. That's all.'

Woodwork class lasted exactly one hour, before we ran to the playground freedom of Saint Joseph's Academy of Hard Knocks, hemmed in on one of its sides by the sandstone blocks of the church nave butting into the play area. We were not allowed to chalk wickets on the church wall – that was tantamount to mortal sin – but we did on school walls. Whoever got to the wicket first batted first, and if one were pretty canny and a good liar, one could keep that wicket for the rest of playtime.

'Don't take that wicket,' said Sullivan. 'It belongs to Jimmy Laverty.'

I was no fool, and I took his diplomatic advice into consideration. Then I discarded it, for the Irish in me said that all things are held in common, and my big brother was as big as Laverty's. Thus I took a stance at Laverty's wicket with the bat I'd kept under the desk.

'Play,' I shouted to anyone who was listening, including Moira McGuinness with her red curls, blue eyes, and spotty face.

'Get off my space,' said Laverty. There he stood, new bat in hand, probably borrowed permanently from a vanquished kid of the lower school, legs astride like Achilles.

'My big brother said that this is common space,' I said with great dignity. 'Play.'

It was then that he hit me on the back of the head with his cricket bat and the common space came up to meet me. Moira McGuinness was helping me up as I howled, holding a great goose egg swelling on my head.

'Play,' said Laverty, stepping across my writhing torso and tossing out an ancient tennis ball to prospective bowlers.

Mrs Irene O'Toole was of fearsome aspect, a shock of burnished red hair tied back from her face with a knotted green scarf, squat of appearance, as Irish as Killarney, walking step by step with great menace, grey eyes staring at the object of her attention, always a great black raincoat covering her ample form like a cloak of repentance. She half shouted when she spoke, but not always, for under the thunder was an angel of mercy. In her hand in the schoolyard she always carried a great gleaming brass bell, which she rang with great vigour when play was over and the prisoners had to return to their jail cells of maths and language.

When I tottered round the corner supported by Moira McGuinness, blood streaming a crimson tide down my face, groaning for the world to hear, Mrs O'Toole swept to my level with commiseration: 'Who was it did this to you?'

I coughed and sputtered, 'Jimmy Laverty.' I didn't care if I was a stool pigeon. I wanted justice.

Laverty was swinging his glorious bat, picking up honorary fours and sixes, lying his way to a whole recess at the wicket. Justice hove on the scene. There was no trial. No interrogation. No defence. No appeal. No jury. Mrs O'Toole swung the bell with a precision that would have been admired by Mr Schwenk.

It struck Laverty between the shoulder blades and his Irish body fell like a stricken ox, like an axed Ponderosa, like day slays night, like Irish drink Guinness.

My head felt so much better.

'She must be a Hun,' said Sullivan.

In the medical room, Miss McNally treated both injured boys with the same compassion, me for my bleeding scalp and Laverty for his concussion.

'You stole Schwenk's drill,' I said to Laverty.

'You're a bloody liar,' said Laverty.

'Sullivan saw you,' I said.

'He's a bloody liar, too,' said Laverty. 'All those Sullivans are.'

When I got into the class late, Mr Jones said, 'What happened to you, Tom Kipper?'

'Laverty hit me with his bat.'

Mr Jones had a lilting Welsh accent, the only teacher it seemed without an Irish name. After I sat down, he said to the class, 'Put down your pens for a moment, boys, and listen to me.'

There was a direct threat of war coming on, he told us, despite a search going on for peace between Mr Chamberlain and Hitler. We must pray harder, pray for peace.

'And while I am addressing you this morning, I have heard reports that some boys are making rude remarks about Mr Schwenk because he is German. I must remind you that Mr Schwenk is a Christian just like you, and even though he would sooner stay in England, his government has ordered him back to Germany. Sit very still at your desks now as we pray for peace and for Mr Schwenk. Brian Haggerty, come up here and read from the Bible. This is Saint Paul's letter to the Corinthians.'

And Haggerty read, 'Last of all, there is faith, hope, and love. And the greatest of these is love.'

'Remember that, boys,' said Mr Jones.

'We're praying for a Hun,' hissed Sullivan. 'Wait 'til me dad hears about this!'

In the next few days, we saw Mr Jones and Mr Schwenk walk together at playtime in the schoolyard, step by step, Schwenk in his worn corduroy jacket with leather at the elbows, thin strands of blond hair blowing across his forehead, Mr Jones taller and more sparse, large framed glasses on his narrow nose, in close conversation under the English overcast sky until breaktime had run out.

'I'm going to pray,' said Moira McGuinness, 'that whichever boy stole Mr Schwenk's drill will return it.'

'Who told you?' asked Sullivan.

'Me brother, Michael – who d'ya think, Paddy Sullivan?'

'Well, let me tell you something, Moira McGuinness, it was Laverty who stole it!'

'Then I shall tell Laverty that he must take it back.' She pursed her rosebud mouth and shook her crimson curls.

'Ha,' said Sullivan. 'And what makes you think a girl could make Laverty be that honest?'

Moira McGuinness just smiled a superior smile, soft crinkles under her blue eyes, that only girls can smile and boys can only wonder at, even in the pilgrimage of their lives, for boys will never understand girls, particularly if they're Irish. It was in the lavatory the following day that Sullivan showed me the stolen drill under his ragged jacket.

The bell rang. 'Laverty gave it to me,' he said.

We filed in and stood behind our workbenches while Mr Schwenk looked through the window, waiting for us to assemble.

Sullivan slipped the drill onto the tool bench as he passed.

'Boys,' said Mr Schwenk, 'I have some good news for some of you.' He looked out of the window and then came back to face us. 'You are to get a new voodvork teacher instead of me. His name is Mr Collard. Bad news for some of you is that he is a very strict disciplinarian, vich I am not. Even though some of you unkindly refer to me as a Hun.'

I'm not sure, but I think he glanced at Sullivan, who was looking angelically towards the ceiling.

'Ah,' he said, striding to the tool bench, 'I see the drill has been returned. Thank you, boys. Now let us continue with our projects.'

We didn't see him the next day.

Someone said uniformed men came to the school to escort him away. And that he was a spy.

'Sullivan,' I said, 'we were wrong about Moira McGuinness. She did talk Laverty into bringing back the drill.'

'Moira McGuinness, me arse,' said Sullivan. 'I beat the shit out of him!'

The church garden was full of daffodils when Mr Jones was conscripted for military service. And my imagination took me to fields far from England and Ireland, where there were disorder, chaos, bravery, and uncertainty, and I wondered if he and Schwenk would ever meet again.

With both of them gone, the school seemed very empty.

I can still hear Haggerty intoning, 'Last of all, there is faith, hope, and love. And the greatest of these is love.'

Neville Chamberlain tottered off the British aircraft full of liverwurst, enigmatic smile on his Old Boy Tory lips, announcing 'Peace for our time', so that the whole of

Europe staggered to a halt, breathing the concept of no more wars to end all wars.

Embassies communicated with each other again. Mr Gerald Forsyth, minor Embassy official stationed in Berlin, wiped his forehead, swallowed another over-brimmed glass of Schnapps, picked up the telephone to call a number in Hofgart Strasse, asked for Fräulein Nebenschnozzer and said, 'It's all right, mein Liebchen, peace for our time. Ich liebe dich.'

She cried in the phone, 'Du wunderbarer Engländer.' And, wonder of wonders, Mr Schwenk, sins forgiven, returned to Hard Knocks.

And there was Hope.

Chapter Five

The Paternoster

'Any man who would propose to that woman would be a saint. And God forgive me for saying that!' said my mother.

'Aye, not a very attractive creature, Mary, but she probably has a good heart,' replied Aunt Sarah.

'Well, she keeps it in her boots! Would you like another drop of tea, Sarah?'

'What is the teacher like, the one who's paying her the attention? Is he Irish?'

'Ah, no, he's an Englishman. Poor fellow. New in the district, probably straight out of the teachers' college.'

'A young man, then, is it?'

'Half her age, most likely. Let's ask Tom. Have you been listening to what we said?' my mother asked as I appeared promptly in the doorway.

'No, Ma.'

'Are you sure?'

'Almost sure.' I nodded a couple of times for emphasis.

'Almost sure, indeed,' she said. 'Now tell your Aunt Sarah and me what Mr Sheffield looks like. Is he young?'

'He's twenty-nine.'

'My God! How did you know that now, child?'

'Well, he was completing a form on his desk and I saw his age. And his middle name's Cuthbert.'

My mother looked at me as though she were seeing me for the first time, and then she looked at Aunt Sarah. 'This child frightens me sometimes,' she said.

When I went out to the park, I said to Sullivan, 'Me ma and Aunt Sarah think that Mr Sheffield is sweet on the gargoyle.'

'Sweet on Spiderlady McCann? Nothing makes me more sick!' Sullivan gave a demonstration of someone in grave peril of being sick while I had to watch until we both laughed. 'Hey, wanna go over to the lake?'

But love is a many splendoured thing, according to the bard, binding the twain in a warp and weft of magic thread, visible to no other eye than that of the lovers.

Spiderlady McCann ruled her classroom like Genghis Khan, adding significance to her every word by twisting her tortured mouth and distending her skinny nostrils as we sat in abject terror, hands on desks where she could see that we were not scratching our beige Irish bodies. That is, until Mr Sheffield arrived. His visits to her classroom came increasingly often, bringing with him papers for her to discuss, or so it appeared. Her demeanour changed just as soon as he knocked on the door and his silhouette appeared through the glazed panels. She simpered coyly, covering her chest with one hand, clutching the swishing cane with the other, jigging from one foot to the next.

'She's got Saint Vitus's Dance,' whispered Sullivan behind me.

'I think she's got fleas,' said Joey O'Brien.

It was a great break for the class; suddenly Spiderlady McCann vanished as we watched an enthralling one-act play starring Lady Juliet McCann and Romeo Sheffield with nuances. The very minute Mr Sheffield bid adieu to his Juliet, Genghis Khan rode again the Steppes, excoriating the peasants of Saint Joseph's Academy of Hard Knocks. But we were interrupted again that fine summer day by Sister Margaret Mary, she of the hazel eyes and angel smile, who gave us our lessons in religious faith. We were all in love with her. Even Joey O'Brien paid attention. All the girls vowed to become nuns just as soon as they could escape their parents.

'The rosary,' said Sister Margaret Mary, 'is the very greatest of all prayers. It was once known as the Paternoster back in the eleventh century. Sometimes fifty or even one hundred Paternosters – Our Fathers – were said on the beads. In the twelfth century, it became the rosary as we know it today.'

'She has grey eyes,' said Sully.

'Hazel like my mother's,' I said.

'Does anybody have a rosary?' asked Sister.

Only Betty McNally had one. Nobody else.

We were Irish. We didn't even have a boiled egg.

'Anything you ask of Our Lady on the rosary,' said Sister Margaret Mary, 'will be granted.'

'Wow!' said Sullivan, whose perception of 'anything' raced post haste to material considerations, like banks.

It was a week later that I found it at a bus shelter. The Hail Marys were of green stone; the Glorias and Our Fathers were gold, the chain silver, and the crucifix polished wood. I'd never seen a rosary like that before. I took it in my hands. The stones seemed soft and warm like a benediction. There was a pretty lady in the shelter wearing a blue raincoat who smiled at me. She looked like Sister Margaret Mary. She didn't say anything when I picked up the beads; she just smiled.

My mother wanted to know where I got it from, as if I'd stolen it. 'You'll have to give it back,' she said. 'Let me look at it again. It looks Irish.'

'Let him keep it,' said my father, putting down his copy of *Das Kapital* next to his breviary.

'There's nobody to give it back to,' I said.

It was a short discussion. I kept it.

'I'm going to pray for something,' I later told Sully.

'Sister Margaret Mary said Paternoster is always answered.'

'She said the rosary prayer.'

'Same thing.'

'What shall I ask for?'

'I wish me dad had a job. You could pray for that, then we'd be rich and could move to another house.'

'Is your house horrible?'

'Me ma says it's only the bugs holding hands that are keeping it up.'

I fingered the beads on the rosary. 'OK. I'll pray for that.'

'Thanks, Kipper.'

'Then I'll pray for a bike.'

'It was on the coach we got,' said my mother, 'thirty-six of us, all members of the Women's Guild, and on climbs Tom Carmody all dressed up with a collar and tie as though he's going to a wake.'

'Did the driver allow him on, now?'

'He always does. Tom Carmody goes on every outing to Wales whether it's Saint Vincent de Paul or the Mothers' Club. He always sits in that seat behind the driver.'

My mother was telling this tale with great drama, between pouring cups of tea, one hand on the pot and the other clutched at her chest. Any moment I expected her to shout, 'Mea maxima culpa!'

'Ah, now, Mary, have a cup of tea yourself.'

'Don't exhaust yourself,' said Uncle Bart.

But Shakespeare was in her blood that afternoon. 'We arrived at the Holy Well and we all got out of the bus to go to Saint Francis Church. Father Doyle led us in a rosary before we retired to the hall for tea. It was Flora Haggerty who said to me, "And where is Tom Carmody?" The man was nowhere in sight and there isn't a pub for miles. So

Flora and I went back to the bus to find poor old Tom asleep in his usual seat with his hat tipped over his head. When I gave him a shake, the hat fell off and Tom fell over, and it was Flora herself who said, "Mary, he's gone home," and there he was, as dead as a Grimsby kipper!'

'Oh, it must have been a fright for you,' said Aunt Moira, snapping another digestive biscuit.

'Father Doyle came out to the coach and all he did was scratch his head and say, "Well now, well now." '

'Not much of a priest for making decisions,' said Bart, scratching his own head. 'No wonder Saint Francis looks like the Salvation Army.'

'It was the driver, Michael Moriarty, who made the decision,' said my mother.

'What decision?' asked Uncle Jack.

'To take him home. But first we continued the outing to Llangollen.'

Bart was laughing. 'You mean to say, Mary, you kept poor Tom Carmody on the bus to Llangollen?'

'Aye. Tom loved Llangollen and we didn't want to deprive him. Michael Moriarty put him comfortably back on his seat with his hat covering those blue Connemara eyes, and off we travelled. We left him in the parking lot before going round the shops and ended up at the Welch Arms for shepherd's pie and a few glasses of wine. When we all boarded the coach to go home, thirty-five of the thirty-six members of the Women's Guild were in their cups.'

'Ah, you were the only sober one, Mary.'

'Not at all. Minny Moriarty, Michael's wife, is a teetotaller. I was just as silly as Lizzy O'Rourke, the president. As we set off, someone suggested we sing to poor old Tom, so we did. We sang to him all the old wartime songs and then some hymns. Minny did a solo of "There's an Old Mill by the Stream" and we cried and it was beautiful.'

'What did you do with Tom?'

'Have another cup of tea, Jack?'

'Yes, please, Mary. Those are good biscuits. What happened to Tom?'

'Well, we all went our separate ways home except for Michael Moriarty, the driver. He was so overcome with emotion about Tom dying on his bus that he went to the Albion for a drink, staying until closing time, and then went home, leaving Tom in the parking lot.'

'You all had a fine time,' said Aunt Moira, pouring the port. Uncle Bart was still laughing.

I was floating on the periphery of the Finnegan gathering, absorbing every gesture of my mother as she related the story and the responses of my uncles and aunts. To me it seemed like a play, where everyone played a part upon the scene of life, those impressions forming images in a young whippersnapper's mind, just waiting to have its pages teeming with script and scene to take to future generations. 'Tom Kipper, go out and play,' said my mother. My espionage was over.

As I skipped through the doorway, I heard Uncle Jack say, 'Hey, Bart, I hear they lost your fine services down at Coastal Shipping.'

'Aye,' said Bart. 'I had a feeling it had run its course, anyway. Some varmint stole twenty cases of whiskey while I was enjoying a bite to eat with the foreman.'

'Why don't you visit your Uncle Xavier?' shouted my mother after me.

'I will,' I shouted back.

It was only many Irish moons later that I discovered the 'varmint' mentioned by Uncle Bart was none other than Conor Boyce. Conor Boyce was 'black Irish', which means different misconceptions depending upon the Irishman you're drinking with and what he thinks you want to hear. An Irishman will delight his listener with a soothing balm of sheer nonsense if that is his wish. The most popular misconception of 'black Irish' – and one in which I myself believe – if you'll relieve my pain with Guinness – is that they are descendants of the Spanish Armada, which was quietly going about its business of invading England when Francis Drake scuttled it. Rumour has it that Drake was Irish, his mother, Madonna Drake, from Kerry. But that's just hearsay.

Conor Boyce was forever painting his coal truck, a most unsightly vehicle, blackened with dust from the rail yard, where Cooley Maginnity ruled until Grandpa Francis Finnegan's dog, Fang, divested him of his trousers. Heaven knows where Conor acquired the paint; it seemed that instead of sluicing the vehicle down with a hose, he painted it. The product of his artistry would never grace the Louvre. A man he never knew at the time, by pure accident, or so it seemed, rubbed elbows with Conor in the Bird in Hand one Saturday night, traces of coal dust still festooning Conor's eyebrows and cap.

'Will you be having one for the throat?' enquired the man. It was pure barrelled Guinness at the Bird in Hand, the magic of the River Liffey: a rare benediction according to old Dan Magonnachy, the world's oldest altar boy.

The man put down his glass in a puddle on the bar. 'Would you be after making a few pounds to tide you and the missus over?'

Conor's eyes glinted under the coal dust, for he sensed the enterprise being offered by his companion was of its nature shifty, full of guile, and delightfully dishonest, but profitable. 'I'm listening,' said Conor Boyce.

'Do you have any red paint?' asked the man.

On Monday afternoon, a driver wearing a bright yellow cap drove a bright red truck into King's Gap loading dock and handed an official pink delivery slip to the assistant foreman for twenty cases of Johnnie Walker Red Label whiskey. The clerk at the desk rubber-stamped the delivery slip and the assistant foreman had the consignment hand-loaded onto the bright red truck, Conor Boyce tipping his bright yellow cap and driving off, wishing everyone the top of the mornin'.

On Tuesday morning, the bookkeeper for the Coastal Shipping Line cried out that two lots of Red Label had been picked up but he had only one delivery slip. The brave constabulary instantly established that a bright red vehicle was involved in the second pickup and the smiling driver wore a bright yellow cap. The foreman was in the pub with Uncle Bart at the time of the aforementioned offence.

'Were there any other distinguishing marks?' asked Inspector Callahan, an Armageddon-faced man from Belfast.

'He had an Irish accent,' said the clerk, Tom O'Neill.

'Don't we all,' laughed Bart, the lunchtime drink being still in him.

And that's how Bart was fired.

Uncle Francis Xavier Finnegan lived on the other side of town, where the grass grew on request, not one whit like Crescent Lane where we lived and fought and dramatised with Irish emotion, slightly off-kilter, but steeped in colour. It was said that he once owned an office cleaning business in the city of Liverpool, and he had the contract for cleaning the windows of the Liver Building. But, my mother intoned, Sinead Finnegan, nee O'Connor, his wife and the love of his life, ran off with that scoundrel, Morty Hooligan, the postman, to Boston, Massachusetts, and was never heard from again.

It was all downhill after that, said my mother, wiping away a tear. So Uncle Xavier bought a house on the other side of town when times were good and washing windows paid a pretty penny. It was a bungalow, sitting prettily in a green garden, surrounded by acacia trees in a row of similar middle-class prosperity and no Irish except Uncle Xavier.

The people on the streets spoke with hot potatoes in

their mouths and all seemed to be looking up at the sky. I unlatched his green gate and trod down his crazy paving to the large glassed-in front door where he met me with his dog, Grip, the most cowardly dog in the world. He was not very large; he was smooth and brown with large brown eyes, and he had yellow fangs through which he snarled with drooled saliva. He looked quite horrible. He fled the instant I touched him with my toe.

'Come on in and be devoured by Grip,' said my Uncle Xavier. Seated in his most splendidly furnished living room, he asked, 'Will it be tea or ice cream, Tom Kipper?' Big chocolate chips stuck out of the ice cream he brought. 'Tell me about all the Finnegan gang,' he said, so I told him about the last gathering on Crescent Lane, the story my mother told about the Ladies' Guild and Tom Carmody in Llangollen. I also told him about Uncle Bart being fired and the twenty cases of Johnnie Walker Red Label Scotch that had vanished. He listened to all I had to say until he had a smile on his face, which was when he looked most like Uncle Bart, his brother. 'Aye, you tell a grand tale, Tom Kipper.'

'I'm saying a rosary to Saint Joseph for you, Uncle Xavier,' I told him.

For a moment he lost his old composure, putting down his pipe that fumed like a broken promise. 'And why on earth would you be doing that, me boy?'

'For a special intention.'

'Which you can't tell me, I suppose.'

'Not very well, Uncle Xavier.'

'That's a fine-looking rosary you've got there; where did it come from?'

'I found it at a bus shelter on Periwinkle Street. It was on the bench in the shelter.'

He fingered the beads. 'And it's on these you're saying this rosary for me?'

'Yes, Uncle Xavier.'

'Then it'll be answered.'

'Uncle Xavier?'

'Yes, Tom?'

'Will you go to Mass with me on Sunday?'

'Ah now, let me think about that, me boy.'

'Me dad got a job. I can't believe it!' shouted Sullivan. 'It's a miracle!'

'What kind of job did he get?'

'Don't know. He got a letter in the post-box. It said he had to report to the box factory at Tollsdale. Me ma's real happy.'

'Better run. We're gonna be late for school and Dracula McCann. Maybe her car will break down,' I said.

'Thanks for saying the Paternoster for me dad.'

It was only then that I remembered falling to sleep praying for Sully's dad with the rosary. I fingered it in my pocket. It seemed to fit into the nooks and crannies. It was peaceful.

'Now, children, I have a very important announcement to make to you. Please put your pencils down and your hands on the desk in front of you.' Four zillion times she has said this. 'One of your teachers is leaving Saint Joseph's – a teacher who will be missed. This is a teacher who has been dedicated to Saint Joseph's students, one whom the whole school knows, and who has had your best interests at heart.'

'It must be "Pop" Devereaux – he's older than the school,' whispered Sullivan.

'This teacher will miss you like a parent misses its children.'

'It can't be Sheffield; he's just arrived,' I whispered from the corner of my mouth.

'There will be a lot of heartache.'

'Maybe it's Sister Margaret Mary.'

Miss McCann touched the moisture at the corner of her eye with a linen handkerchief. 'This teacher will be missed.' There was a knock at the door. Mr Sheffield's silhouette was framed against the frosted glass briefly before he walked in.

'It's Romeo,' hissed Sully. 'Now we'll never know who she's talking about.'

'Good morning, Miss McCann.' His salute was jovial.

'Good morning, Mr Sheffield,' blushed Genghis Khan.

'Have you heard the news, students?' asked the beaming Mr Sheffield. 'Has Miss McCann told you? Well, I'm sure she won't mind my telling you that Miss McCann and I are to be married.' He was dancing. Wait 'til Ma hears about this.

'He's mad,' said Sullivan.

'Bonkers,' said O'Rourke, who never said anything.

53

'Off his rocker,' said Laverty.

'However, children, I have a piece of sad news for you after that positively splendid good news.'

'What is it, sir?' yawned Joey O'Brien from his Isle of Elba desk in the back row.

'Miss McCann is leaving Saint Joseph's!' said Mr Sheffield.

A great stillness settled on Saint Joseph's Academy of Hard Knocks, a shroud of quiescence muffled all sound, the tatty pigeons in the belfry cooed not, all articulation was extinguished, and the earth ceased to tremble.

Then Kipper, Sullivan, O'Brien, Laverty, O'Rourke and Casey, and the Hollihans, Noonans and McCoys all raised their arms and hands to heaven and shouted, 'Yahoo!'

Sully Sullivan and I looked at each other in utter joy.

'It was the Paternoster,' said Sullivan.

He was smiling the broadest Irish smile I've ever seen him smile. 'She's coming home,' said Uncle X. 'She's coming home. My Sinead is coming back from Boston, back to me, Tom Kipper, and it's all thanks to the rosary you said for that special intention!'

'But, Uncle X!'

'Aye, it's all right, lad, now I know what you've been praying for. To Mass it is I'm going with you on Sunday,' he smiled. 'Now here's a little gift.' Into my hands he pressed a pound note and then another, crackling, it seemed to me, like logs in a furnace.

First, Sully's dad got a job. Second, Genghis Khan is leaving, and now Uncle X is going back to church. He thinks I said the rosary that Aunt Sinead would return from Boston. What could I say? The two pound notes were snug in my pocket. My heart was singing.

'What are you smiling at?' queried my mother. She fretted if we laughed, and she fretted if we cried.

'Uncle X is going to Mass with me on Sunday.'

'What is it you're saying now?'

'Uncle Frank Xavier is going to Mass on Sunday.'

'The Lord be praised! How do you know this?'

'He told me.'

'You saw him?'

'I went to his house.'

'Why would he tell you such a thing?'

'It's the Paternoster,' I said.

'What in the wide world are you talking about now, Tom Kipper?'

'I prayed the Irish rosary for him.'

'Does he know that?'

'I told him. Guess what else!'

'What is it now?'

'Auntie Sinead is coming back to him from Boston.'

'Holy Mary!' My mother put her hands on the back of the chair, sat down, and raised her apron to her face. 'Did he tell you this, Tom Kipper, or has your imagination gone quite mad?'

'It's true, Ma!'

She put her hand on my shoulder. 'Listen to me, now:

55

run over to your Aunt Moira's and tell her the news. Tell
her she'd better come on over to see me. Then run and tell
Bart. Glory be praised! Tell Bart to bring a bottle of that
whiskey, the Red Label.'

'Red Label?'

'Never you mind. Just tell him. It'll still leave nine
cases.'

And that's how I found out about the red truck and the
most mysterious case of the missing Johnnie Walker Red
Label. It was a grand meeting. Even Uncle X came. There
seemed to be more than an adequate supply of whiskey
brought by Uncle Bartholomew, and the talk was all about
Auntie Sinead. Uncle X beamed.

'And Miss McCann has left you?' asked Aunt Moira.
'With the English teacher. Was he smiling now?'

'He won't be smiling long,' said my mother, and the
whole company tumbled over with laughter.

It was the following day that the great drama overcame
me in County Park, for in reaching in my pocket I found
the Irish rosary was gone. High and low I searched the
lakeside area and the cricket pitch and the Pavilion
grounds until the sun had set. As I raced to cut through
the rose garden on my way home, clouds scudded
overhead in the twilight. The figure I passed turned to
look at me at the end of the pathway. It was the pretty
lady in the blue raincoat I had seen at the bus shelter. She
smiled and was gone.

My mother would have boxed my ears, but she knew
the Paternoster, as I still called it, was gone, so she made

me a special cup of tea instead. 'There now,' she said, fretting.

Sully said, 'Well, you found it; now somebody else will find it.'

'Do you know,' I said, 'the only thing I didn't get was the bike.'

'You can have my bike,' said Sully.

'You don't have a bike.'

'At the chandler's. The delivery bike. It has five speeds and the loudest bell on Merseyside.'

'But how can I have the chandler's bike?'

'I'm offering you the job, Tom Kipper. Me dad is making firewood chips in the backyard and he wants me as his assistant. More money.'

'Wow! How much does it pay?'

'Five bob a week. You work after school and on Saturday mornings.'

I shouldn't have hesitated. Every kid was looking for a good job. 'You better make up your mind fast, Tom Kipper. She asked me to get someone to take my place.'

'Where is it?'

'It's next to the fire station on Reeds Lane.'

'That's miles away!'

'You get the carrier bike, dummy!'

My world suddenly changed. A bike! It was like being offered my own aeroplane. I had made my own bike from scraps, a rusted frame from the junkyard, handlebars 'borrowed' from the Salvation Army, wheels minus half the spokes discarded in an alley, inner tubes more porous than a loofah, and a leather seat to blunt your buttocks. It was minus brakes. To bring this unconventional vehicle to a stop, the driver placed a foot on the moving front wheel. One day, proceeding at a rapid pace down Saint Hilary's Brow, a sharp, cobbled incline, I had practised this latter manoeuvre, the brave rider (me) being launched over the vehicle onto the cobbles, where he bled ingloriously for a while before limping home, leaving the crumpled vehicle where it lay.

'When do I begin?' I asked Paddy Sullivan.

I went along with him on Saturday morning to the Charming Chandler next to the fire station. 'How long do you have to go before you leave school?' asked Fiona Jenkins.

'Six months, miss,' I answered.

It was a good bike with a carrier on the front, onto which I loaded fire starters, cans of paraffin, soaps, and brushes. Off I'd pedal to local houses, meeting mostly young housewives in dressing gowns who treated me as if I were a very special individual with an important job.

When I was not at school or working, I rode that bike everywhere; we became almost one being. I polished it daily and locked it up at night.

It gleamed in the moonlight.

So I got my bike after all!

Before falling asleep at night, I often wonder who found the Paternoster.

Chapter Six

Spyglass Hill

'Liverpool,' said Mr Schwenk, 'reminds me of Hamburg.'

Mr York adjusted the pipe in his teeth. 'I hope you're not taking pictures back to the Fatherland, Carl,' he replied. They looked at each other momentarily and then laughed. Conversation had been overcast with the impending return of Schwenk to Schleswig Holstein. None of the teaching staff at Saint Joseph's wanted him to leave, but he had shown them during one lunch break the letter from Berlin to all German nationals abroad.

The maths master, Gilbert Hooley, stood alone and resolute. 'Good riddance,' he sputtered. 'Bloody good riddance.'

'Oh, come on, Gilbert,' said Mr York, 'Schwenk is a damn nice chap. He's just caught up in circumstances beyond his control.'

'He's a Hun,' said Hooley.

'And you're a bloody Irishman,' said Mr Dylan Kingsley.

'From Southern Ireland,' added Pat Trimble, the music teacher.

Schwenk and York walked across the larger of the asphalt playgrounds, stepping across puddles left by the previous night's rain. 'I don't really want to go,' sighed Schwenk, 'but my family is back there and they also expect me to return.'

'Are you worried about them, Carl?'

'No, not really. There are just my mother and father. My two brothers are caught up in the swastika euphoria.'

'Then don't go,' said Fred York.

Schwenk looked alarmed. 'I'd be interned,' he said.

'So?' answered Mr York.

'I may even be thought of as dappling in espionage.'

'You, a spy?' York laughed.

'I am afraid, Mr York. For the first time in my life I'm afraid.'

'Then think about what I said.'

In July there was a small tea party in the teachers' conference room for Carl Schwenk before he departed England's pastures green. The headmaster, Edward Swift, addressed the gathered faculty and said pleasant things about him and how he had discharged his duties well, and that we were all Christians who should pray for each other, particularly in these uncertain times. Even Hooley shook his hand.

Pat Trimble, the music teacher, cried as the faculty sang

'For He's a Jolly Good Fellow'. Mr York took him in his Triumph to the train station in Liverpool.

The last anybody saw of him was as the Triumph rolled through the school gates and down Wheatland Lane. Our teacher for the day, Mr Wilson, allowed us to stand at the schoolroom window to wave to the passing car.

'Come on, boys,' he said, 'back to good old arithmetic.'

We all groaned.

'Me dad and me,' said Patrick Kinneally, 'saw the ghost.'

'What did he look like?'

'Well, we didn't see him properly.'

'How did you see him then?'

'Kind of like a white face at the window.'

'Which window?'

'A bedroom window, upstairs.'

'How high?'

'Two floors up.'

'You're a liar, Kinneally!'

'Honest. It's true.'

'How can you see a ghost two floors up, all that distance away on the Hill? That's impossible!'

'Well, we did. Ask me dad.'

I said I didn't believe him, but I did.

It was called Radcliffe Manor, a glossy, red-bricked mansion on the side of Spyglass Hill, with turrets, gables, and a plenitude of windows, now all shuttered on the bottom level but big and vacant on the two top storeys. It looked friendly but lonely, musing like a lover without his true love, softer in the summer and bleak in winter, with leaves chasing the wind by its closed doors. With the threat of war brewing on the Continent, the Radcliffes had departed for Australia, so the house was shuttered, the weeds grew, and the ghost arrived, for no respectable rambling mansion is complete until it is favoured by a lonely spirit moving within its walls. And no spectre is complete without a legend.

Kinneally wrote his essay about the Radcliffe ghost, for the assignment was that we could write an essay about any subject matter we liked. Kinneally sharpened his pencil on the Radcliffe ghost behind the windowpane, he of the white face and staring eyes who had been left behind by the Radcliffes to guard their property on the Hill. It was whispered in the village that old Radcliffe had brought back voodoo magic with him from the Congo.

Mr York laughed out loud when he read the essay, awarding Kinneally high marks for his imagination and inventiveness. I was most annoyed about this because Kinneally was a lousy speller, but he had the Irish in him.

'Mr York,' said Betsy Braddock, 'goes up to Radcliffe Manor on Spyglass Hill every month at five o'clock on the first Saturday.'

Kinneally and I looked at her with utter astonishment.

Betsy Braddock always looked prim and neat and tidy, with clean, polished black shoes and white stockings, her red hair tied back on her head in a gleaming ponytail. She was always right, was Betsy Braddock; information disseminated by her was never in error. That's why we boys groaned whenever she proved herself implacably right.

'To see the ghost, I suppose,' said Kinneally.

'No, Patrick Kinneally,' sniffed Betsy, 'just to check on Radcliffe Manor for Mr and Mrs Radcliffe in Australia.' She walked away with her nose in the air.

'Let's kick her in the shins,' said Kinneally, but he didn't mean it. 'I've got a plan.' He told me what was festering in his wild Irish mind, and I didn't like it. But I went anyway.

It was about three or four miles up to Spyglass Hill; we took the trail beside the old GWR railway track, past fields full of blackberry, hawthorn, and ponds green and smelly, alive with frogs, in an English summer that seemed to have no end. Way in the background we could see Spyglass Hill with the weather-stained sandstone observatory on its summit, steeped in trees, the dome with glinting black glass shutters.

'Where does your pa work?' asked Kinneally.

'He doesn't. Doesn't believe in it. He has what he calls a philosophy,' I answered.

'What's a philosophy?'

'Dunno. He just doesn't work.' We were quiet for a while. 'I think it's something to do with Karl Marx,' I added.

'Who does he play for?'

'Nobody. He doesn't work either.'

* * *

Miss Pat Trimble, music and drama teacher, exactly forty-one years of age, lived with her ageless mother in a quaint, feminine cottage named Villa Monticelli on Cobblestone Drive. Leaving Saint Joseph's Academy of Hard Knocks and driving her minuscule Morris Minor home at 4:30 P.M. to Cobblestone Drive was like switching countries, for the ancient red-bricked school lay entrenched in the glut of working-class Blotchley, while Cobblestone moved at the pace of the upper-middle class with lawns. The cottage contained no counter or window ledge that was not festooned with bric-a-brac: porcelain ducks, swans, and geese; countless miniature cottages like Villa Monticelli; vases; and statues of Saint Joseph all picked up on trips to Welsh valleys or Continental spas.

'I know you're in love,' said Mrs Patricia Trimble to her daughter, Miss Pat Trimble. 'I was once in love myself with your father, the beastly man.'

'Mother, please don't say that about Daddy. And I'm not in love. I am not married, and never will be. And I'm not even engaged.'

'He was Irish,' said Mrs Trimble. 'No wonder he was beastly!'

'Mother!' She laced up her walking shoes. 'I'm going over to the drama club.'

'Pour me a glass of sherry before you go, darling, and stay away from those beastly actors.'

* * *

Spyglass Hill, with its windmill on the peak of the northern abutment and red sandstone cliffs worn and modelled by ancient years of rain and wind, was a magnet to Patrick Kinneally and Tom Kipper.

'We'll look for the ghost later,' I shouted.

We didn't know the day was closing down until the sun burned red briefly through the tattered angry clouds and raindrops spattered on our faces. Down through the fern we scrambled, down Spyglass Hill with rain trickling through the old oaks, onto the rutted track, and down to the village drive, which bordered the gated entrance to Radcliffe Manor.

'Where's the ghost?' I asked.

'You see that window up there at the end of the roof? That's where we saw the white face.'

'Can't see anything in this rain. It's getting dark. C'mon, we better go home.'

'Wait just a minute,' said Kinneally.

A mist was drifting from the steaming heather, and raindrops pattered across us gently. A figure moved by the big front entrance gates, one hand holding on to a metal rail, the other drawing a hood closer to its face. He or she was waiting for someone to come down to the gate.

'Look,' breathed Patrick Kinneally in a frightened voice.

A pale yellow light flickered in the window, throwing a moving shadow against the blind. The light glowed brighter before dying out. 'I told you so. It's the bloody ghost.'

My feet wouldn't move. 'The door's opening,' I said. Down the pathway in deepening gloom hurried the shadowy shape of a man, moving towards the great iron gate with urgency. We could hear his feet scuff on the wet pavement. He was wearing a heavy-looking raincoat and hat so that we could not see his face in the gloom. The ornate gate opened and the man and woman embraced in the teeming rain, locked together like one figure.

'My darling,' she kept saying.

Kinneally and I kept looking at each other behind the shrubs, staring wild-eyed in wonder at what we had stumbled upon, for we were innocent but felt guilty, caught unsuspecting in dark intrigue.

The two figures moved together to Radcliffe Manor's front doors, clinging in embrace, hid in the shadows and disappeared.

'It's Mr York,' I said.

'It's the spirit,' said Kinneally.

'Spirits don't say I love you.'

'How d'ya know it's Mr York?'

'Betsy Braddock said he had the key, and today's the first Saturday of the month, isn't it?'

'But he's married.'

We let that piece of information hang in the air, suspended for some time in the innocence of childhood, which was not dispelled until we found it funny.

At the bottom of the Hill on Village Drive was parked a small car near the gate. 'It's Miss Trimble's car,' I said in awe.

'Miss Trimble kissy-kissy with Mr York,' said Kinneally. 'Wait till me dad hears about this.'

'No, no, you can't tell him,' I said.

'Why not?'

'I dunno. It wouldn't be right. It's a secret.'

'Let's get home. I'm soaking wet. Me ma's gonna kill me.'

'Me too.'

We looked back at Radcliffe Manor, but there was no light in the window; the spirit slept.

When the bombing started, it changed our lives. 'It's called the Blitz,' said Jimmy Laverty. Large-scale evacuation of children to the colonies took place, to Australia, New Zealand, South Africa, Canada, and even America.

When the Blitz hurried itself from southern England to the Midlands and northwest, Blotchley became as bomb-battered as any other town adjacent to industry, which was when the Red Cross saw Radcliffe Manor as a splendid HQ for the General Blotchley District.

Gilbert Hooley, maths teacher extraordinaire, pain in the nether anatomical dispensation, became post president of the Civilian Defence Force. When he espied Radcliffe Manor with its cavernous interior and botanical location, he drooled with utter joy, for he despised with great anguish the Radcliffes, who were Tories while he was Irish Labour, not quite red but a healthy pink. Bureaucratic wheels were set in motion.

Mr York was summoned to the headmaster's office in

the middle of class to speak with Mr Gilbert Hooley, post president of the Civilian Defence Force.

'Radcliffe Manor,' said Mr Hooley, 'is a vacant possession that has been declared a most acceptable location for the CDF, what with the air raids becoming increasingly more numerous and the CDF needing a central headquarters.'

'Radcliffe Manor,' said Fred York, 'belongs to that family and no one else.'

'I am advised that you have a key, access to the Manor.'

'That is indeed true. Now excuse me – my class is unattended.'

'You don't understand, Mr York. We have been given official permission to occupy these premises for defence purposes. Please give me the key.'

'Never in a month of Sundays,' swore Fred York, slamming the door.

Betsy Braddock had a tartan bonnet on her head and on her face was a most superior smile.

'She's coming to tell us something,' said Seamus McCarthy.

'Why is she looking so happy?' asked Tom Cavanagh.

'Because it's something nasty,' answered Vincent Quinlan.

'What do you want, Betsy Braddock?' I asked.

'If you don't want me to tell you, Tom Kipper, I won't.'

We all remained silent. Why stem the tide of oft-times valuable information? 'Have the Germans surrendered?' I asked. 'Aye now, don't walk away, Betsy,' I ventured as she turned on her heel. 'We were just having fun.'

'Well,' she said, 'next Saturday they're going to break down the doors of Radcliffe Manor!'

'Who's they?'

'Mr Hooley and the CDF.'

'Who told you that?'

'My mother – and she knows everything.' She did, too. She was a one-woman propaganda ministry.

'What time?' I asked, glancing at Kinneally.

'Twelve o'clock.'

'But what about the ghost?' asked Kinneally.

'There's no ghost, silly. There's no such thing!'

'Mr York won't let them in,' I told Kinneally later on. 'They say he has refused to give them the key.'

Six of us hiked the GWR track the following Saturday. The Saint Thomas Church clock in the village was striking the half-hour when we arrived to join some people from Blotchley and some from the village to witness the grand entrance.

But there was none – no trumpets, no bugles, no splendid speeches – just Mr Gilbert Hooley, a short, red-haired man in overalls with a pair of wire cutters, and a policeman, Sergeant Dan O'Rourke of the village constabulary. When Saint Thomas struck noon, the red-haired man in the overalls placed the cutters round a chain holding a lock and snipped. The chain fell away, but the gate did not open. The red-haired man then took a bunch of large keys from his belt, inserted them one by one into the gate lock, and at key number four the gates swung wide open. There was a cry of delight and the small crowd pushed forward. 'No,' shouted Mr Hooley, 'only officials allowed in the grounds.' It was to no avail, for Radcliffe Manor was the stuff of legend, and the peons were not to be denied a peek into the battlements of the aristocracy.

And, no doubt, they would have gladly broken down the massive entrance doors for Mr Hooley and the CDF, but they were halted on the steps by Mr York himself, who was holding a brass key aloft.

'Look,' said Kinneally. 'Here comes Miss Trimble and Mr York.'

'I shall open the doors,' announced Mr York, 'even though I despise your gaining entrance to private property.'

Someone shouted, 'There's a war on!'

Mr York slipped the brass key into the lock and slowly opened the grand doors, which moved easily on silent hinges to reveal a spacious entrance hall with a gleaming parquet floor, an arched ceiling flooded with light, gilded handsome mirrors, and the figure of a man seated at a small ornate table, drinking tea from a china cup.

The man stood up as Mr Hooley entered, followed by everybody who could crowd inside.

'Who the devil are you, sir?' asked Hooley.

'Vy, don't you recognise me, Mr Hooley?'

'My God,' said Hooley. 'It's Schwenk!'

Pat Trimble was pushing her way through the crowd,

then broke into a stumbling run.

'Darling,' she sobbed. Then she and Carl Schwenk were in each other's arms amid sobs of delight. Some applause started among the visitors.

'This is ridiculous,' snarled Old Hooley. He then turned to Sergeant O'Rourke, saying, 'That man is a German spy!'

'Is this true, sir?' asked O'Rourke, touching his hat.

'No, Sergeant, it is not true. It is true that I am German, but it is not true that I am a spy.'

'He's a teacher from Saint Joseph's,' said Mr York.

'Would you mind answering a few questions down at the station later on, sir?'

'Not at all, Sergeant; I would be delighted. Would it be all right if I brought along Miss Trimble, my fiancée?'

'That'll be quite all right, sir. We'll have a nice cup of tea.'

My mother, Mary Catherine Kipper, said, 'Mr York must have been feeding him and allowing that Trimble woman into the mansion.'

'It's a love story,' said my father, burying himself in *The Pickwick Papers*.

My mother, Mary Catherine Kipper, nee Finnegan, stared at him over her glasses. 'And how would you know, Mr Karl Marx?'

It was the middle of the week, and Miss Trimble had just come to visit Mr York at his desk. Jimmy Laverty raised his hand to ask a question. Mr York nodded.

'Please, sir, will Mr Schwenk be executed as a spy?'

'This is a history class, Jimmy Laverty, not a discussion on espionage.' He slapped the desk with his cane, the one he used to knock common sense into Irish Catholic heads. 'However, seeing that you have asked the question and seeing you all evidently want to know, no, he will not be executed. He is being held as an enemy alien at a POW camp in Wales.' He had a faraway look in his eyes. 'We may visit him next month. What do you think of that?' We cheered and banged our desks. In a conspiratorial voice, he said, 'We may even take Miss Trimble with us.'

Pat Trimble blushed with elation.

That evening she started her letter: 'My dearest Carl, We all love you, even the boys at Saint Joseph's. Let me tell you what Mr York said today . . .'

Kinneally said to me, 'Hey, Kipper, let's go up to Spyglass Hill on Saturday and look for the ghost.'

'Yeah!'

Chapter Seven

The Old Fellow

'The Old Fellow' always wore fireman's braces holding up his 'trousers'; that's the way I remember him when I get a mental vision of him going out into the backyard to till vegetables or steal coal. When he put his thumbs behind those suspenders and screwed his mouth around, I knew the Old Fellow was in the throes of generating income. I never referred to him as the Old Fellow, of course; that was reserved for Uncle Bart and his two brothers, Aloysius and Xavier Finnegan. The Old Fellow's name was Francis, and his three daughters called him Pa. I called him Grandpa and I was his favourite, which was why I got to stay at his flat for weekends and sometimes longer if he needed me as a decoy when he became a subsidiary associate of the coal industry without their blessing.

From his coal industry expertise, Grandpa was able to finance his fondness for weekend pints at the two local pubs he loved, the Bird in Hand and the Dirty Duck, both with the aroma of stale beer, sawdust, and creaky pine floorboards. Not to mention educational seminars on how to make the price of a pint, at which Grandpa was an acknowledged master. When he spoke on such matters, which was not too frequently, everybody put down his glass and cocked his antennae, for Grandpa's word was pure gold. On the subject of stealing coal, he had a PhD.

'He's going to get caught one fine day,' said my mother to her two sisters, Moira and Madge, over a large pot of fragrant tea and buttered scones. It was at this point that she told me to go outside and play in case I became educated in the matter of Grandpa's exciting industry, little realising that I was privy to all camps and that my grey matter was absolutely crammed with every finely sifted piece of data upon the matter. Besides which an ancient bottle of port had miraculously appeared on the kitchen table and 'the girls' were embroiled in a little friendly discussion on the morals of Mrs Maggie Malone, the widow in the next flat. I liked the Widow, as they called her, for every so often she would give me a penny or a bar of chocolate, always with a smile on her gypsy face that I could never quite understand. She was Grandpa's finest customer. A large percentage of his net worth came from the Widow.

'We'll catch his ass one fine day,' said Railroad Inspector Cooley Maginnity, echoing my mother's sentiments, over a pint of foaming ale at the Dirty Duck. His cronies nodded in their beer, bought for them by

Maginnity, the authority on the seizure of criminals at the rail yard. 'The coal he takes,' he said, 'should be firin' up the furnaces of honest industry.' Grandpa, over at the Bird in Hand, was laughing in his Irish whiskey, for there were twenty-four hours in the day, the night-time of which was when he, Francis Finnegan, moved in the shadows like the elusive Pimpernel.

Grandpa's flat, where he lived with Aunt Moira, was in a row of other flats that lay parallel with the goods train railway siding. The big red engine would bring in the train of box cars with the open tops full to the brim with coal, uncouple it and leave it sometimes for many nights behind the fence that separated the railway tracks from the row of flats. It would take an agile person to climb that fence, steal coal, and get back to the safety of his own backyard before he was caught by Inspector Cooley Maginnity, who had X-ray vision, they said.

But Maginnity was no match for Francis Finnegan, bald of head, bleary blue eyes, big buckled belt round his middle supported by his fireman's braces, for he was a will-o'-the-wisp, as elusive as a good intention, a phantom, a transient image, an unincorporated coal industry. However, Maginnity was a bitter man but sharp, hostile but cunning, resentful but shrewd, callous but crafty, and there came a day when my grandpa disappeared for five days. I was so used to almost living at Aunt Moira's flat that I could not understand where he had gone. My aunts would give me no answer when I enquired, and neither would my mother; and as my father was still studying dialectic materialism with Karl Marx, he was no help. But Grandpa came home after five days and was very quiet. I heard him in his bedroom saying his Hail Marys and rattling his beads, but he didn't go down to the Bird in Hand or the Dirty Duck. I was putting minuscule shards of data together to solve this mystery when my suspicions were confirmed in the playground.

The Maginnity kids were big, with their shoulders bursting out of their Saint Vincent de Paul shirts, and they were pretty mean, light in the mind, and heavy in the hand. I grabbed hold of Patrick Maginnity by the front of his shirt. 'What did you say about my grandpa?'

'He just spent a week in jail, shrimp, and let go of my shirt!' To make sure I did, he swept me off like a fly.

I tried to clobber him, but he just donged me with a fist as big as County Cork, and I lay on the playground looking for my big brother, Quentin, to help me with the Maginnity war that had just started.

'And another thing, shrimp,' said Patrick Maginnity, 'my pa put him in the slammer. Ha. Ha. Ha.' And the three Maginnity kids went away, chortling their heads off.

'Don't you ever say that again,' remonstrated my mother when I told her. 'Your grandpa is a fine man. He probably went to see his relatives in Connemara.'

'I thought he came from Dublin.'

'Connemara, Dublin – what does it matter? Now off you go to school or you'll get your ears boxed by Miss McCann.'

I couldn't believe that Maginnity had outfoxed

Grandpa. I was almost his aide-de-camp. We had been defeated in battle.

During the time he had been AWOL for five days, I had taken care of Fang, the half-German shepherd that Grandpa kept in the backyard for fear that he might attack the populace. Fang was fearsome of aspect, slavering constantly at the black jowls, and grinding his adenoids deep in his throat, his front teeth very large and razor sharp. But he was a pussycat with Grandpa and with me, for he would squeal with delight when I played with him, even when he knocked me down in the radish beds with his massive bulk. Grandpa would get annoyed for just a fraction of a second, for I was his favourite and I couldn't do much wrong.

'Where did you get the black eye?' he asked.

'At school, Grandpa.'

'Did you respond?'

'It was a big Maginnity kid.'

'Maginnity?'

'Yes, he said his dad put you in jail.'

'Did he now.' He pulled at his braces and screwed his lips around, which was when I started to feel better, for I knew the signs of impending combat.

I can see the Old Fellow now as I did through the upper bedroom window as he bent his Irish back to the shovel, neatly arranging the excavated soil on three sides of the shaft. 'If you can't go over, you've got to go under,' he said to me in the drizzle, his yellow sou'wester gleaming with rain. He knew he had an intimate relationship with me; my lips were sealed, for the very same dark Gaelic blood coursed through our veins, not to mention a trace of larceny.

When he finished and when the trap door with its camouflage of sodden grass was in place, the enemy would never have envisioned that a short tunnel in red clay led to black coal, heaped invitingly just outside Francis Finnegan's back door. His commerce recommenced although the operation proceeded at a much greater rate of knots, speed being the key factor in outwitting Maginnity. As Grandpa pulled the very last piece of coal through the tunnel, he sealed his exit with a large, grey boulder, which fitted with great exactness its required purpose.

Then the illegal cargo was spirited into the night to clients who slept in their beds with the satisfying knowledge that their coal bins would be full the following morn. Maginnity raged at the Dirty Duck and Grandpa laughed at the Bird in Hand, while it became the subject of lively conversation at both seedy taverns.

Meanwhile, Grandpa flew the Irish flag every morning from a pole he had constructed many years before, borrowed for some time, he said, from a police yard. Maginnity stepped up his surveillance, convinced that if he took the railroad siding section by section in the night, he would eventually discover the means by which railway coal was being systematically depleted. He thought that it could not possibly be by Grandpa, even though that was his first thought, for he could not espy any ascending ladders over the fence, and what other way could the coal bandit have access?

Over at the coal office, Valentine Banahan worked the heavy ledgers, keeping count of inward and outward freight, scornful of the loud, aggressive Maginnity, who sneeringly called him 'Mr Valentino'.

At the Bird in Hand, it was Valentine Banahan who rubbed shoulders with Grandpa Finnegan and whispered over the black porter, 'He's doing your section tonight,' which was when Grandpa bought him another pint as he expanded his empire into espionage.

It was a black night with no rain, a moon that flitted from behind a dark mantle from time to time, a night fit for Irish fairies and Cooley Maginnity with a lantern in his hand and darkness in his heart. He heaved his bulk across the sloping mound of grass and shrub bordering Grandpa's flat until he came across the huge grey boulder, the one that fitted so snugly at the tunnel exit. He cast his lantern on the rock and pushed it this way and that until it moved to reveal a chasm, an opening, and he gave a great whoop of sheer joy. Down went the lantern on the ground, and with two hairy hands he pushed the grey boulder aside, which was when Fang struck. With an awful, horrifying howl that would strike terror into the heart of any man, Fang launched himself, jaws agape, slavering jowls at Inspector Cooley Maginnity, sending him spinning down the embankment. With a speed beyond his years, he gained his balance and fled in terror pursued by Fang, who caught him at the signal, fastening those razor teeth upon the seat of his uniformed pants.

Fang tore and Maginnity pulled, but in opposite directions, and when this unseemly battle arrived at a grand finale, Cooley Maginnity fled down the rest of the railroad track minus pants, while Fang Finnegan proudly padded back through the tunnel to present Grandpa with his prize. Quickly Grandpa worked on his preconceived plan, filling back the tunnel, pulling back the rock, smoothing out the turf, planting radish where there had been none before, and retiring, sore with laughing, to bed. I even heard him laughing in his sleep.

The following day the sun shone. It was Sunday, and we all went down to Mass at Saint Joseph's, me with Grandpa who carried his tattered missal with the Gaelic script on the flyleaf.

At the Bird in Hand that night, Grandpa was offered several free pints, which he accepted gracefully. There was great laughter in that seedy tavern, for the word had spread, and men and women came from blocks around to see Grandpa's flagpole, at the top of which were flying Cooley Maginnity's trousers. It was many, many years later that I came back from America and saw the picture of the Old Fellow hanging in the bar of the Bird in Hand.

And you know what?

I had tears in my eyes.

Chapter Eight

Always
Great Expectations

'What, may I ask,' said my mother, Mary Catherine Kipper (nee Finnegan), 'are you going to do about these letters?' She took the bowl under her arm and whisked the mixture with a stout wooden spoon.

My father, self-confessed philanthropist, albeit permanently unemployable, sprinkled dark, angry-looking tobacco into a Rizla paper, licked it, rolled the ends together, and said, 'Nothing!'

'Another one came this morning,' she said.

'That'll be twenty-two,' he smiled through an early morning grey stubble.

'The law will put you in jail,' said my mother, just to test his reaction.

'The law,' said my father, who lived in a Dickensian

world of his own choosing, 'is an ass!'

'So you're going to do nothing?'

'Karl Marx said that oft times doing nothing is doing something, and in this he was supported by Engels.'

'Well, you're going to have to do something this time; you have to appear in the magistrates' court next Tuesday.' She triumphantly handed him letter number twenty-two. He peered through his wire-rimmed glasses and moved his mouth this way and that.

'Perhaps,' said Mary Catherine Kipper, 'Karl Marx can defend you, supported by this fellow Engels.'

'Quiet, woman,' he said, 'while I think,' which he did, falling asleep in the process.

I was a consummate reader; I read labels on clothing; liquor advertisements; margarine wrappers; bits from the worn, leather-covered Bible; certificates for all manner of consumables; letters that my mother kept from Ireland in a top bureau drawer; and my dad's summons to appear in the magistrates' court the following Tuesday, which gripped me in curious fascination. 'Why is Dad going to court, Ma?'

'In answer to a summons,' she said.

'Did he steal something?'

'What a question to ask, Tom Kipper! Of course not!'

'Then why is he going?'

'He missed a payment on his Dickens Library.'

It was so exciting. My whole family was into larceny. Grandpa was into coal. Uncle Bart was into kippers. And now Dad was into books.

But to miss just one payment and have to go to jail seemed illogical, so I read through all the other twenty-one demands for payment for a super deluxe, leather-bound, gold-lettered library of Charles Dickens. Among the personally antiquated Kipper family furnishings, the elegant case enclosing the Dickens Library stood in high relief, gold letters on red leather, the handsome books already well used by my father, who could quote cast, characters, texts, and conversations on request.

Dad couldn't screw in a light bulb, but he walked with Wilkins Micawber and spoke with Little Dorrit and ambled with Mr Pickwick.

He also hadn't missed one payment; he'd missed twenty-two.

'Hey, Uncle Bart,' said my younger brother Vincent, when Bart came to call on his sister, my mother, 'me dad's going to jail!'

For this impetuous petty peccadillo he received a clip across the ear from my mother. 'Do not be impudent,' she said, 'or you'll sip sorrow with a long spoon, young man!'

'What's happening, Mary?' enquired Uncle Bart, his curiosity piqued by the word 'jail', which he had squeaked by like a shadow most of his colourful life.

Over a cup of strong, sugared tea, my mother revealed my father's impending visit to the magistrates' court the following Tuesday at ten o'clock in the morning. 'What will I do, Bart, if he lands in prison?'

'I'll send him a file in a Cornish pasty,' laughed Bart.

'I'll think about it next Tuesday, I suppose,' said my

mother. 'And what do YOU want?' she said, turning to me.

'Can me and Paddy Sullivan go hiking up Windward Hill tomorrow after school, Ma?'

'Well, all right, but you have to take Vincent.'

'Aw, Ma!'

The day we went scrumping was one of those rare English summer days when earth and sky and lake and stream, daffodil, sweet williams, balmy air, nettle rash, and Mrs Donohue came together with a policeman to arrest us.

'Let's go gorging,' said Paddy Sullivan. 'Gorging' was local patois for stealing apples – red, green, and yellow with shiny ripe coats, hanging in orchards just waiting to be plundered, and for Irish kids to do the plundering.

'There's an orchard,' said Frank Murphy, 'down in the village behind Saint Hilary's, with thousands of apples. Thousands!' Now, Sullivan's deliverances of what purported to be fact were always met with great scepticism, but Frank Murphy's were nothing but the truth. Our mouths watered at the mere dream of one thousand apples.

'Vincent has to come along,' I said.

'Your brother Vincent?' groaned Sullivan.

'Well, your brother Sean's coming along, too!' I pointed out.

'Yeah, but he's bigger and can run fast.'

'What does that have to do with it?'

The five of us went.

The village was two miles away by a lazy country road

along which we blissfully walked and ran and scrambled and were in heaven. At the end of it lay a thousand apples, which were not ours, and therefore infinitely desirable. At the end of the lane, I stopped and said to Vincent, 'If we get caught, give them a false name.'

'What d'ya mean?'

'If someone asks you your name, don't tell them you're Vincent Kipper. Tell them you're Vincent Smith.'

'Vincent Smith?'

'Yes. And if they ask the name of your school, tell them it's Bramdale.'

'But it's Saint Joseph's.'

'We know that, dummy, but tell them it's Bramdale.'

'OK.'

'I'll be Peter Smith.'

'I'll be Andy Jones,' said Paddy Sullivan.

'And I'll be Bill Jones,' said Sean Sullivan.

'And I'll be John Daley,' said Frank Murphy.

'And we all live on Primrose Lane but with the wrong numbers. OK?'

'OK,' all the espionage agents agreed. Very sharp fellows, with false identities we were eager to take on the world of adults who disturbed our equilibrium.

'Here it is,' said Murphy.

'It's behind a wall,' said Sullivan.

'That wall's too high,' said Kipper, which was me.

There was a shop in front, out on the main roadway, with the rear garden extending behind it down a narrow side street. A red brick wall bordered the garden, and it was formidable. Two large old apple trees stood majestically behind that wall, and they held the delight of five Irish urchins upon their boughs, one thousand glowing pippins of red and green and streaky yellow.

'The wall,' said Murphy, 'is lower this end.'

Thus began the siege.

Up the narrow ledge we went and onto the steep end like Vikings, pulling luscious apples as fast as we went, dropping them down on the grass verge below where we would gather the harvest before leaving the village with all speed. Mrs Irene Donohue, widow of some ten summers, proprietor of Ye Olde Chandler Shoppe, owner of one thousand apples in early stages of depletion, put down her opera glasses at the rear window and dialled the village constabulary, which consisted of two policemen, Sergeant O'Driscoll and Constable Fogarty.

'Mr Fogarty,' said Irene Donohue, 'there are four or five boys taking my apples.'

'Do you recognise them, Mrs Donohue?'

'I don't think they're from the village.'

'I'll be right over now.'

Constable Fogarty slipped down the lane on his issue bicycle with great stealth, braking to a halt at a brick wall swarming with industrious apple pickers.

'It's a copper,' said Murphy.

'On a bike,' said Sullivan.

'Get down here now, you boys,' said Fogarty.

Slowly assembled against the wall, the five espionage agents stood in a litter of plucked pippins.

'Names?' said the constable, pulling a notebook from a top pocket. 'You first,' he ordered, pointing a large pencil at Paddy Sullivan.

'Andy Jones,' said Sullivan.

'What's your school?'

'Bramdale.'

'Address?'

'26 Primrose Lane.'

'And you?'

'John Daley,' said Frank Murphy. 'Bramdale School.'

'Where do you live?'

'31 Primrose Lane.'

'Peter Smith,' I said, in answer to his question. 'Bramdale, 43 Primrose Lane.'

Sean Sullivan's alias was Bill Jones, Bramdale, and Primrose. We gave each other shifty glances.

Fogarty was filling his official journal with splendid precision, five youthful prisoners on whose parents he would call with great pomp to illuminate their criminal history.

To the fifth and final prisoner he said, 'And what's your name, young man?'

'Vincent Kipper,' said Vincent Kipper.

'Same school?'

'Saint Joseph's.'

'You bloody rat!' whispered Sullivan.

'I'll kill him,' I said. 'Me own brother!'

'After me,' said Murphy.

'All you kids look Irish,' said Constable Fogarty.

* * *

On the memorable Tuesday morning, my father was singing 'Glory Hallelujah!' and was in a buoyant mood.

'I can't go to the magistrates' court, can I, Ma?' I asked.

'No, you can't. Off you go.'

Saint Joseph's Academy of Hard Knocks was a zillion miles away. The whole family knew the day: Uncle Bart, Uncle Aloysius, Uncle Xavier, Aunt Madge, Aunt Moira, and Grandpa Finnegan, all of them tumbling over each other to the magistrates' court. It seemed to me that I was the only one excluded from this spontaneous gathering of the clans, thirsting for blood.

So by degrees, by prodding, by eavesdropping, and by absorbing as only a thirsting child can, I gathered the unfolding story between the clatter of teacups, laughter, and exclamations.

The collections agent, a Robert Wiggins of Crabtree & Wiggins, gave testimony that some two years before, Joseph Kipper had agreed to purchase by mail, on a monthly payment system, a library of books by author Charles Dickens. He had not made one payment since the agreement was signed. Value of the said library: one hundred and seventy-five pounds, plus interest.

'Is the foregoing testimony true, Mr Kipper?' asked Judge Fortesque Morehead, addressing the accused.

'Yes, Your Honour, every word of it.'

The judge perched like a raven on the bench. He had a large beaky nose, Uncle Bart said, which he was always blowing, and he had watery blue eyes.

'Why did you make no payments, Mr Kipper?'

'Because I have no money, Your Honour.'

'Are you unemployed?'

'Yes, Your Honour.'

'What is your profession, Mr Kipper?'

'I'm a philanthropist and philosopher, Your Honour.'

'Indeed!' Judge Fortesque Morehead allowed himself his daily smile. 'And do these professions respond financially to your needs?'

'Only should the recipient of my benefactions consider them of worth.'

The judge's eyes were now open. Droves of penniless working-class dross came through his chambers, awed by their surroundings and his exalted honour in his white wig and shrouding gown. But here was Joseph Kipper, unemployed, unembarrassed, suave, and foxy.

'Let me ask you, Mr Kipper: have you read these novels by Charles Dickens?' His Honour was now ready to deliver the *coup de grâce* to his opponent.

'All of them, Your Honour.'

'All?' He leaned back in his insignia-embossed chair. 'Can you name some of them?'

'I can name all of them.'

A titter went up from Aunt Madge.

'I would like to hear them, Mr Kipper.'

'Certainly. *Pickwick Papers*, *Sketches by Boz*, *David Copperfield*, *Oliver Twist*, *Bleak House*, *Little Dorrit*, *Great Expectations*, *Our Mutual Friend* – shall I continue, Your Honour?'

'No, that will suffice. Do you know the characters?'

'All of them.'

'Would you care to elaborate?'

And Joseph Kipper did.

His Honour Fortesque Morehead was now leaning forward on his desk. 'Tell me about *Little Dorrit*,' he said quietly, and Joseph Kipper did.

And the room was hushed. And tears formed in the eyes of Fortesque Morehead. Aunt Madge, of emotional nature, was heard to sniffle. And when Joseph Kipper came to a conclusion, there was a great silence in the courtroom.

'Mr Wiggins,' said the judge, 'when you sold this library to Mr Kipper, did you first enquire of his financial ability to pay?'

'Mr Kipper conducted correspondence with my client, Your Honour, from which it was presumed he was financially able.'

'Presumption, Mr Wiggins, has brought you a creditor. Mr Kipper,' said Judge Fortesque Morehead, 'under the circumstances involved in this transaction, I must find you guilty!'

Aunt Madge wept.

Uncle Xavier shouted, 'Damnation!'

Grandpa Finnegan said, 'Shame!'

The judge said, 'I therefore order you to pay this account to Crabtree and Wiggins at the rate of one penny per year!' With that, he banged his gavel. And then my father rose to his feet and shouted, 'And I'm not going to pay that, either!'

There was great celebration in that seedy tavern, the Bird in Hand, that night; my father, the Ragged Trousered Philanthropist, carried the day, declared there should always be *Great Expectations*, and drank everything.

The following day, Wednesday, Constable Fogarty was invited into the parlour, as were Tom Kipper and his scroungy brother, Vincent, whom we afterwards christened 'Loose Lips'. My dad's singular disdain for the ass of the law precluded him from entering the room, so my mother sat to listen to the young constable, blue helmet on his knee, tell of the false names and addresses he had been given. 'The only real honest lad,' said Constable Fogarty, 'was your boy, Vincent.'

Vincent cringed, praised by a 'copper', condemned to death by his brother, with excruciating torture.

'Will you be having a cup of tea, Constable?' fussed my mother.

'Aye, I will, Mrs Kipper. It's a hot day.'

It was raining cats and dogs.

She gave him a cup of flavourful tea and a plate of her best chocolate biscuits, putting his helmet on the sideboard. 'Isn't your mother Fiona Fogarty?' she asked. 'She used to be Fiona Blackwell?'

'That's right, Mrs Kipper. How did you know?'

'We went to Saint Joseph's together. She was in a higher grade than I was, with Mrs McCabe.'

'That's right again, Mrs Kipper. We moved to the village about ten years ago.'

Two more cups of tea later, Constable Fogarty had completed his important civic chore. Sergeant O'Driscoll would be pleased with his sterling report. 'Stealing apples led to telling lies,' he said to me.

My mother said, 'His father will chastise him. Right now he's in correspondence.' He was fast asleep.

'Good day to you, Mrs Kipper.'

'Give my regards to Fiona, your mother, Constable.'

'I will, Mrs Kipper.' He adjusted his helmet and rode off on his issue bicycle down Primrose Lane, full of tea and chocolate biscuits, looking for criminals.

'Tom Kipper,' said my mother, 'wait 'til your father hears about this!'

'Hey, Ma, before you tell Dad, are we Irish?'

'As sure as the good Lord and His Blessed Mother are in heaven!'

'Is Kipper an Irish name?'

'The Kippers,' she said, stirring her tea, 'and the Finnegans were famous in the scourge of the potato famine in the last century. Why, they almost ate the very last potato stolen from the mouths of the English landlords before sailing for America.' She sniffed at the thought of her illustrious forebears.

'Dad says we're descendants of the Norman Conquest and we have royal blood coursing through our veins.'

'He does, does he! Well, tell him it's Irish potatoes that are feeding his royal blood.'

'If the Kippers and the Finnegans went to America, why did we come to England?'

'Well, now, it was a tragedy. Your great-grandfather, Padraic Finnegan, God rest his soul, stopped over at Liverpool and was unjustly accused of stealing whiskey – and he as honest a man as ever trod the streets of Dublin – so they held him over so long he eventually became a policeman.'

'Ma, a lot of Irish became policemen, didn't they?'

'Aye, policemen, poets, priests, politicians, and maybe one day Pope. They practically rule the world.'

'Isn't it great to be Irish, Ma?'

'Aye, it is, my boy – one day you'll get to that blessed island.'

'Ma?'

'Yes?'

'When I go to confession, will I have to tell about the apples?'

'Of course you will!'

'But I didn't actually take any.'

'Ah, yes, but you had the intention.'

'Ma.'

'Yes?'

'When Dad bought the library, did he have any intentions?'

'Tom Kipper! Why don't you go out to play?'

'OK, Ma.'

When I got outside, Paddy Sullivan was eating a big apple.

Chapter Nine

*A Smack
in the Kisser*

Charity O'Brien was a misfit. A charm of a young woman, she was from Galway. She worked as a 'cleaning lady' at Saint Joseph's Academy of Hard Knocks.

But Charity longed for the 'owld' country across the Irish Sea, for she did not find the streets paved with gold in England as the song had promised, and although England was green enough, it wasn't kelly green.

'Have you thought of going back?' asked my mother, Mary Catherine Kipper (neé Finnegan), pouring steaming water into an English blue porcelain teapot.

'Nobody wants me,' said Charity.

'Have you got no family then?'

'All gone to America or London, except for those gone home,' she answered, looking at the ceiling.

Aunt Florence, who had brought the apple pie that I liked, said, 'Could you not go to Galway yourself then, Charity, and find some kind of lodging house, perhaps a nice landlady and a job at the local school?'

'There's no jobs,' she said, and that was final, for that's why the Irish came to England, starting with the potato famine. It was at Liverpool that most of them caught a ship for Ellis Island two hundred years ago. And it was in Liverpool that many of them stayed, including my great-grandfather on my mother's side, Padraic Finnegan, a giant of a man and a great Latin scholar to boot, according to my mother, that is. Uncle Bart used to laugh at this. 'A giant? He was shorter than me and the only word he could spell was beer.'

'Ah, Bart, now,' responded my mother, 'stop filling the child's head with Irish nonsense. He was almost an Irish king!'

All the kids in my school had Irish names, most of them starting with the letter 'O' followed by an apostrophe. Our name, Kipper, was looked upon as English even though it had an Irish ring to it.

'Will you be having some of this apple pie?' asked Aunt Florence of Charity O'Brien.

It was only later on when I was eavesdropping that I heard Uncle Bart say to my mother, 'She's a fine-looking woman of only nineteen summers if she's a day, that Charity. Should find herself a good husband instead of drooling like a sick hen about the old country. Could you lend me half a crown, Mary?'

'Aye,' said my mother, 'but where will she find a good-looking Irishman this side of the water, Bart? No, I can't; you'll only spend it on beer.'

But she gave him the half-crown anyway, and off he went to the Bird in Hand, a crumbling, white-walled pub on King Street, steamy with the odour of stale beer and tobacco, plots against the English realm, and Irish laughter. It was almost a shrine. We passed it every bright, shining morning on the way to school, the odour of pale ale in our nostrils, the battered door of the pub shut tight against the very last drunken Irishman to exit. It held mysteries for us, like a castle in the Irish mist, for we wondered pensively why men in cloth caps and scarves made so much noise in that darkened interior and slurped so much foul beer. Uncle Bart was a prince in that castle, mostly because of his double-headed penny. At two-up, you can't very well lose with equipment like that.

When Matthew duMaurier first came to school, he stood out like a Kerryman without porter. His new shoes shone, he wore a tie, he was well barbered with hair parted at the side, and he was clean as a whistle – not at all like the ragged urchins surrounding him. He had no holes in his elbows and spoke with money in his voice. Worst of all, he came in a car.

'Look at this,' said Sully, pulling me to the railed fence that separated us from the civilisation of Hilary Lane. The car pulled into the teachers' parking lot. A pink, well-dressed lady wearing an oversized lace bonnet bent down to kiss a very clean boy on the cheek.

'Ugh!' said Sully, which meant that this kid was going to get a smack on the kisser.

The very clean boy ventured to the periphery of the whirling melange of screaming adolescence as his mother, as we thought, drove out of the lot in her lace bonnet.

'Let's push him over,' said Sully, which he did.

Matthew duMaurier didn't understand this at first; the laws governing Saint Joseph's Academy of Hard Knocks were wholly incomprehensible to him. He just sat in the grit of the schoolyard holding his backside, looking pained and viewing the world in horizontal wonder.

Charity O'Brien, the cleaning lady, who was passing by, started to pick him up when Mrs O'Toole, jangling her great school bell, came full steam across the yard.

'Here comes the albatross,' said Sully.

'What are you doing down there, boy?' she crowed at Matthew duMaurier. 'Get up on your feet. You're new here, aren't you? Go over to the school office and register. Who did this to you?' She looked over her shoulder at Sullivan and then rang the bell for classes. She knew it was Sully, and she would exact justice later with the subtlety of a bulldozer. There would be no trial. Sully called it revenge.

It was later on that Sully said, 'I'm going to take revenge,' digging his fists into his pants pockets and sneering.

'On who?'

'On a crabby old lady.'

'How can you take revenge on an old lady?' I asked. 'And you can't take revenge anyway.'

'Who said I can't?'

'It's in the Bible. Sister Marion said so.'

'I don't believe it.'

'She says that the Bible says, "Vengeance is mine, sayeth the Lord." '

'Mrs O'Toole takes revenge.'

'How come?'

'Didn't you see her whack me yesterday?'

'Yes, Sully, but that's not revenge.'

'Well, what is it then?'

'It's what you get for smacking somebody else in the kisser!'

'It's revenge. So, if she can take it, so can I. Last Saturday we saw *The Man in the Iron Mask* and he got his revenge.'

'He did?'

'He was really the king of all France, and his name was Philippe, but his rotten brother, Louis the Fourteenth, had him thrown into jail.'

'What for?'

'Because he wanted to be king, so he had an iron mask fitted to Philippe's head so no one could recognise him.'

'Then what happened?' I asked, mentally conjuring up my brother Jack having an iron mask fitted to me and throwing me into a closet.

'Philippe escaped and took his revenge.'

'He killed Louis the Fourteenth?'

'No, even better – he had an iron mask fitted to him and threw him into a black pit in the Bastille. That was his revenge!' Sullivan dug his hands even deeper into his pockets and continued to sneer.

'Where are you taking this revenge, anyway?'

'Come on, I'll show you.'

The brick house at the northern end of Hazelwood Drive was sunk in spacious green lawns and russet trees. Wrought iron fences that were not unfriendly surmounted the low terracotta walls on all sides except the north, where it abutted Lowland Crescent. It was over this wall that we went, Sully and I, he cajoling me into a backdrop of his revenge.

'But why are we coming here?' I whispered into his ear, brushing away leafy lavatera branches.

'Because there's no fence.'

Before I could grapple with this inane comment, Sully had pushed up a small window as though he had done it before, and I was climbing in after him. He closed the window inside the kitchen. 'They've gone away to the country until the Blitz is over.'

He was talking quite loudly while I whispered, 'I hope we don't get caught!' I blessed myself.

'Nah,' said Sully.

I became caught up in the character of the house. It was the biggest I had ever been in. I should never have followed Sully. We crept into rooms that to me were dazzlingly splendid. The walls seemed to be plastered with portraits of important people in gilded frames, only one or two smiling – most of them seemed to me to be angling their bodies or faces as though, in Sullivan's words, they had a scratchy arse.

Racing through my mind all the time was *The people who live here must be the aristocrats that Mr York told us about in our history lessons.* 'Hey, Sully,' I said. 'Let's get out of here.'

'I want my revenge first,' said Sully.

A clock bonged the three-quarters hour over in the next room, it seemed, which is where Sully swiftly headed.

The fireplace filled out a snug hollow in the far wall, the hearth full of brass and pewter fire irons, the mantel shelf surmounted by a clock with a gleaming ebony case, the face with clear, black Roman numerals, and the fingers artistically scrolled to final points. It was handsome, as handsome as the lady in the blue dress in the picture above, who seemed to be smiling at the two Irish urchins in her handsome house.

Sully reached up and took the clock. 'Let's go,' he said and headed swiftly through the passageways with me on his tail, scared to death.

'Close the window,' he breathed as I tumbled through. We could see no one in Lowland Crescent through the lavatera, so we climbed over the wall, the clock under Sully's ragged coat like a parcel of bricks, breathing hard, walking at a trot down to the dell and into the trees where the clock bonged the hour of four and gave us a fright.

'I've got some chewing gum,' said Sully, giving me a piece.

'Did you get your revenge?' I asked him eventually as we sat on the damp grass, chewing the sugary gum.

'I got the clock for me ma,' he said. 'That's my revenge.'

'How come?' I asked him quietly.

'Me ma came home one night,' he told me. 'She was carrying a bag and she tipped out some clothes on the kitchen table as she was mad as hell. Me dad didn't have a job, so she got one as a cleaning lady for Mrs Fossingham.'

'Who's Mrs Fossingham?'

'She's the woman whose house we just broke into.' Sully had a tear in his eye. 'When she'd finished cleaning the house, Mrs Fossing-arse gave me ma some old clothes to pay her for cleaning all day. Said the clothes were worth more than the money. That's why I took the clock.'

I looked up at the clouds scudding across the English sky. 'Will you sell it?'

'No, I'm gonna give it to me ma.'

'So that's your revenge against Mrs Fossing-arse!' I laughed.

'Yeah,' he said, 'the English bitch!'

Matthew duMaurier had a brother with the name of Raymond who was drafted for military service during the 'Emergency'. Unlike most young men from upper-class society, he abhorred the idea of handling firearms close up or from long distance, so when confronted by the draft board, he said, 'I want to be a coal miner, thank you.' He was on sound legal footing in making this decision, but the president of the board said, 'I see your father was a full colonel in the last war, Mr duMaurier,' and in a short space of time, Raymond became a second lieutenant in an infantry regiment. He came home on leave one English summer day prior to embarking for overseas. It was then that he met Charity O'Brien, who opened the front door to let him in. His buttons gleamed, he carried a stick and leather gloves, and a pencil-thin moustache dashed across his upper lip.

'Is Mother home?' he asked; then he was gone to the rear of the house where he knew she would be.

'He's either Errol Flynn or Robert Taylor,' said Charity to herself.

Before dinner that evening, Raymond said to his younger brother, Matthew, 'Where did Charity come from?'

'From my school. They call it Saint Joseph's Academy of Hard Knocks because it's so tough. One of the other students, a kid named Sullivan, knocked me down on my first day and Charity picked me up. I told Mother, so Mother found out where she lived and brought her home.'

'She's Irish?'

'As Irish as Daddy. She's from Galway, which is where Grandfather is from. Why did you want to know this stuff?'

'Because you're telling me.'

'You're daft!'

A ten-day leave from the Army is to be savoured. The mere contemplation weeks before brought a large smile to Second Lieutenant Raymond duMaurier whenever he drank a cup of scalding tea in the officers' mess or returned the salute of two passing corporals who thought he was a shit. All of his contemporaries from Oxford days were likewise pretending to be gentlemen in His Majesty's Armed Forces, so that two days into his ten-day furlough, ennui crept into his psyche like a kipper in a drizzle. Meanwhile, he was up here in the northwest where duMaurier Industries laid its head, while most of his friends were a stone's throw from Piccadilly Circus.

On the third day, he took Charity O'Brien up Windmill Hill for a jaunt in his father's car, although his father never knew it. Neither did his mater.

The fourth day he kissed her. The fifth day she kissed him. Charity O'Brien came out of her shell like Irish blarney from O'Reilly's bar.

It was a bad day at Saint Joseph's Academy of Hard Knocks when one bright spring day Mr Fisk, Mr Geoffrey Fisk, suffered a verbal drumming from his good – some say otherwise – wife, Veronica Fisk, nee Snodgrass. He then drove to the dingy part of the town where we lived and dreamed and decided he would spill his venom on Sullivan. We answered the register, and Fisk took off his glasses and said, 'I cannot bear the sight of an uncombed child; that is why I have removed my spectacles.' We waited. 'Francis Sullivan,' he said, 'we didn't comb our hair this morning, did we?'

Sullivan didn't say anything. His shock of red, almost orange hair was a matted jungle.

'Have we lost our tongue, Francis Sullivan?'

Still nothing from Sully.

'Come here,' said Fisk.

Sullivan walked to Fisk's desk.

'Do you have a comb, Mr Sullivan?'

'No.'

'No, what?'

'No, I don't have a comb.'

This enraged Fisk. 'Does any boy or girl in this class have a large comb, large enough for Mr Sullivan's head?'

The forty kids in the class laughed nervously. Angela Fitzpatrick said, 'I have,' and she lifted up a long green comb while she covered her mouth with her other hand to stop from giggling.

'Go out to the washroom,' said Fisk, 'both of you, and come back with our hair combed.'

Sully and Angela left the room while Mr Fisk felt much better about the drumming he had received earlier in the day from Veronica Fisk, nee Snodgrass. It felt almost like revenge. When Sully returned, he was a changed kid. There was a parting on one side of his head with hair slicked down on either side in orange waves. Freckles danced on his red face, but he was not smiling. All the girls in the front benches oohed and aahed.

Sitting next to me, Sullivan said from the corner of his mouth, 'I'm gonna get me revenge!'

'He's as Irish as Paddy's pig,' said my mother, 'which is more than I can say for that Mrs duMaurier with her large English nose in the air.'

'How can anyone be Irish with a name like duMaurier?' asked Auntie Cynthia Sweeney, nee Kipper.

'Ah, Cynthia, now, there are fine Irish names like Devereaux and Eamonn de Valera, the finest Irishman who ever lived apart from Saint Patrick, which may sound French but are as Irish as the shamrock. Mr duMaurier is from the self-same place as Charity O'Brien. Could be kin for all you know.' She drank some tea and continued with her knitting.

'Saint Patrick,' said my father from the depths of his big, scroungy armchair, 'was an Englishman.' My father was allowed one sentence a day. That was it.

My mother just continued knitting furiously. 'Take no notice of him,' she said. 'He's an Englishman.'

'Ma,' I said.

'What is it now?'

'I was talking to Matthew today in the school yard.'

'Matthew who?'

'Matthew duMaurier.'

'You were, child? What were you talking about?'

Auntie Cynthia Sweeney said, 'Is that the younger duMaurier boy?'

'Paddy Sullivan bashed him,' I said.

'Now why would he do a thing like that?' asked my mother, giving me a beady eye.

'Sully said he was a sissy.'

'Indeed, and what did the duMaurier boy do?'

'Well, Auntie Charity came along and picked him up.'

My mother was all attention now. 'You're talking about Charity O'Brien now?'

'Yes. You told me to call her Auntie Charity.'

'Well, never mind about that. So she picked up the poor child?'

'Yes, and now she's working on Windmill Hill.'

'Who is?'

'Auntie Charity.'

'Working where?'

'At the duMaurier manor house.'

'Glory be, child! Why didn't you tell me this?'

'Well, Ma, I'm telling you.'

'Listen to me now. How long has she been on the Hill?' My mother took my arm. I was a gold mine for the gossip corporation.

'Don't know. About a month, I think.'

'Heavens to Murgatroyd! Aye, small wonder we haven't seen hide nor hair of her these past few weeks.'

'They're gonna get married.'

My mother's eyes were slate grey. At that moment they looked like quarry yards. 'Who's getting married?' She was shaking me. I weighed about forty pounds after ice cream. I rattled.

'Auntie Charity and Raymond duMaurier. They're in love. Matthew told me.'

'And who is Raymond duMaurier?'

'Matthew's brother.'

'Glory be,' said my mother again. She was utterly speechless until I pried her fingers from round my arm.

When Uncle Bart paid his daily visit, my mother told him breathlessly of the unusual betrothal. 'That's the boy in the Irish Guards,' said Bart. 'He'll be good for a pint at the Bird.'

'Is she doing the right thing, Bart, d'ya think?'

'Marrying into all that money, Mary. What if Joe had been so wealthy?'

'You mean the ragged trousered philanthropist. He's just gone to look for a job in the park.'

The duMaurier wedding was a grand celebration at Saint Joseph's. Money on 'The Hill' thought it odd that one of their people should celebrate in the guts of Chipton-Downs instead of at the Anglican high church at Todbury, which was of sufficient elevation above sea level to be considered a local call to sublime exaltation.

Even the Kippers and the Sullivans were invited. Charity duMaurier, nee O'Brien, was a picture in white lace, Raymond in his Guards uniform. Mrs duMaurier was not as snotty as my ma had said, for they spoke for some time at the reception in the village hall over wedding cake. I thought many days later that my ears were deceiving me when my ma said to Auntie Madge, 'A fine being, that duMaurier woman. I'm sure she must be Irish.'

All the school's teachers were present, including Mrs O'Toole, incomplete without her great bell, and Mr Geoffrey Fisk, science master, sniffing at Sullivan as he passed with a large plate of iced cake. But he did not leave Saint Joseph's parking lot to ride home in his Rover car that day. He had four flat tyres. Sullivan had his revenge.

It was well over twenty years later that I went to England on my vacation and bumped into the youngest duMaurier, Matthew, who was now Father Matthew, five years out of an Irish seminary and assistant at Saint Joseph's, where I attended Mass the day after my arrival. The church hadn't changed one bit; my initials were still visible third row from the back on the Blessed Mother's side where I had handcrafted them with a blunt penknife.

Mr Raymond and Mrs Charity duMaurier, nee O'Brien, now had five rowdy kids in steps and stairs and still lived up on the Hill near the windmill.

Quite by chance I also bumped into Sullivan at a church function, a picnic in the local park not far from the cricket pavilion. He wore a uniform. He was now Police Inspector Sullivan.

'Stolen any good clocks lately, Sully?' I asked.

And he said, 'Kipper, how would you like a good smack in the kisser?'

Chapter Ten

Quentin Sullivan

Mad Harry Flanagan lived in the next-to-end house on Turpentine Drive. 'He became a recluse after his foin wife, Moira Mulcahey, passed on to the good Lord.'

'What's a recluse, Ma?'

'Like a hermit living in a cave. Something like your father,' she said, looking down her Irish nose at me dad, who was reading Karl Marx in his favourite armchair. 'Cut himself off from the world, he did. I think he was once in the Legion of Mary. Anyway, he just stopped talking to people – wouldn't even return the time of day. When people attempt to speak to him, he makes noises.'

'What kind of noises?'

'Your father says it's a cross between begorrah and marmalade. Ah, poor man that he is, we should say the rosary for him.'

'Why is he called Mad Harry?'

'Aye, it's full of questions you are, Tom Kipper. Isn't it time for school?'

That was the combined knowledge Sully and I had of Mad Harry Flanagan until one day, straight after school, Mad Harry Flanagan slipped on the pavement in the rain, just round the corner from Atwright's Fruit Shop after purchasing an extra-large bag of apples. The apples spilled out from Mad Harry's recumbent frame like scattered marbles. Pedestrians who knew of Harry's bizarre personality picked their way around him, while a pack of Irish-faced kids ran past shouting, 'Mad Harry, Mad Harry!'

'Let's help him,' I said.

'He's wacko,' said Sullivan.

We looked at each other. 'The Good Samaritan,' we said, almost together, for Sister Goodchild had spoken to us that very morning in our religion class.

We picked up the green apples one by one from the pavement and gutter, putting them in Harry's sack while he climbed to his feet with the aid of a stick.

'I live just down here,' he said. 'Will you carry the apples to the house for me?' He limped. When he got to his feet, we noticed that he was pretty tall and heavy-looking, bigger even than Sully's dad, Quentin Sullivan.

'He's crackers,' Sully whispered to me.

'Come on in, lads.' He held the door open. The room inside looked bright and colourful. 'It's only a small house but it was enough for Moira and me.'

A brown grained portrait of a young woman in floral

dress, skirt to the ankles and large floppy bonnet in her hand, looked out from above the mantel. 'That's me wife who's gone to the Lord,' he said. She looked back at us. 'Be nice to him,' she seemed to be saying.

'D'ya want some tea, lads?'

'We've got to be going, Mr Flanagan.'

'Oh, you know my name, then?' We didn't answer. 'Tell me about your school,' he said. 'I used to have a lad like you once.'

It seemed we were mesmerised into staying. He produced delicious chocolate eclairs and hot, steaming tea in no time, which tasted all the more scrumptious, for rain was bouncing hard now against the parlour window. It was difficult for Sully to keep still in his seat at the tiny table, for he was still sore from the caning given him by Mr Wilford Bromley, geography and history master. 'What's the matter, lad?' asked Mad Harry, and Sully told him.

When we eventually left the little house, Harry said, 'I used to know your mother, Sully, from many years back. Now you boys drop by here any time you like. People think I'm mad, but it's just that I don't want to talk to anyone. But you're different. You were like the Good Samaritan to me.' We were goggle-eyed. That's just what Sister Goodchild had been teaching us and what we remembered before helping Mad Harry.

When I got home, my mother said, 'You went into the home of Harry Flanagan? Tom Kipper, if you do that again, I'll box your ears.'

'He gave us tea and chocolate eclairs, Ma.'

'I don't want to hear one more word.'

'OK, Ma.'

'Where did he get the eclairs from?'

'I don't know.'

'What did you say the picture was like, the one of his wife, Moira? Did he use bad language? Did he put sugar in the tea? What did he talk about?'

'He said he knew Sully's mother.'

'What was that? Knew Mrs Sullivan? Heavens to Murgatroyd, why don't you tell me these things?'

'I'm trying, Ma.'

'Don't be cheeky. You're getting more like your English father every day. I must drop in to see Mrs Sullivan when I go to the market tomorrow.' Then she almost whispered, 'Who can understand or appreciate the fine Irish mind!'

Sully's family lived down Pinafore Lane, not far from Saint Joseph's Academy of Hard Knocks. Their home was crumbling, old red brick, small and square, two storeys, tightly mortared together with a dozen others, like dirty urchins viewing the middle distance because there was nowhere else. He took me home after school where I was greeted by the Sullivan smell – not quite aromatic, not offensive, but a lived-in smell, vapours that told of a tribe communal, Irish, a genuine, comfortable smell, generous and giving.

''Ello, Tom, will you 'ave a cuppa tea?' asked his mother.

'Yes, please, Mrs Sullivan.'

'And how's your mother?'

'Fine, Mrs Sullivan.'

'Will you be having one of these chocolate biscuits?'

'Thanks, Mrs Sullivan.'

'Has your dad got a job yet?'

'No, not yet. He's still looking, I think.'

'Where's me dad?' asked Sully.

'He's gone down to the police station to talk to the inspector.' Mr Sullivan was a big knot of a man from Cork. He boxed heavyweight, they said in the 'owld' country, but he lost every round to his wife, Sarah Sullivan, nee Considine.

Mrs Sullivan gave me the tea in a big fat cup, chipped at the lip, accompanied by a saucer of a different pattern, chipped by Michelangelo. It was a warm, comfortable cup, not unlike Mrs Sullivan herself, embracing the lender and the borrower.

'Why is he talking to the inspector, Ma?'

'Well, he's proving to him that he was nowhere near the school when Mr Bromley was assaulted.'

'I thought he told that to the policeman who called.'

'That he did, but he wasn't believed.'

'Was that when you accidentally spilled the hot cup of tea in his lap, Ma?' asked Sully, smiling.

'Aye, it was, lad. A genuine accident, to be sure.'

'Tell him to jump in the lake, Ma.'

'Well, now, I did. In a manner of speaking.'

* * *

It was fascinating to all us kids at Saint Joseph's Academy of Hard Knocks, for a few days earlier, Sully had been beaten across his backside with a cane by Mr Wilford Bromley, the geography and history master. That evening it seemed twilight descended earlier than usual, married to an English mist from the river, so that when Mr Bromley stepped through the school yard after tidying his desk, a large figure slid wraith-like through the fading light to thwack Mr Bromley across the side of his head with a heavy stick, awarding him with four stitches at Memorial Park Hospital, a stone's throw from where Sully and I fished for tiddlers.

The *Chipton-Downs Post* reported in the following issue that the assailant whispered in the victim's ear, 'Don't hit the boys!' Then he was gone. Wilford Bromley could recollect no description. Unfortunately, being a history master, he said something rather nebulous about the Scarlet Pimpernel, which the editor of the *Chipton-Downs Post*, starved for news, jumped upon with great delight.

The English teacher, Francis Chumley, asked Bromley at tea break if the Scarlet Pimpernel wore a mask, weak but sly English humour not appreciated by Bromley, who was furious as he coughed in his tea.

'Aren't you going to Miss Stapleton's?' asked my mother.

I wheeled the delivery bike out of the red flagged yard and cycled with a joyous feeling of speed to the Charming Chandler on Mulberry Street. I was occupied there part-time delivering fire starters, soap, paraffin, matches, glue, and any kind of miscellaneous chandlery to executives' wives who lived in middle-class splendour in Chipton-Downs where no one was Irish but everyone spoke good English.

Miss Dolores Stapleton said, 'Tommy, there are five deliveries in the store room. Take them one at a time. You were late today. What happened?'

'I was with Mad Harry Flanagan.'

'Oh.' Miss Stapleton didn't hear what I said. She was in love.

It was starting to get dusk when I delivered the last package. Wilford Bromley, history and geography, opened the brass-knockered door of number twelve, Blotchley Crescent.

'Who is it, Wilford?'

'It's the delivery boy from Stapleton's.'

'Have him bring the box in.'

'What's your name, boy?' He didn't recognise me.

'Tom Kipper, sir.'

'Well, you most probably attend Harrogate Avenue Elementary. Much better, no doubt, than that Saint Joseph's.'

'Darling, don't talk to the boy like that.'

When Mr Bromley turned his head, I saw a large strip of medical plaster stuck on its top where the Scarlet Pimpernel had struck his blow for justice.

'Give the boy sixpence, Wilford.'

'Here,' he said. But all he gave me was a threepenny bit.

'Can I have the box back, please, sir?'

'Yes, go on, take it.'

When I saw Sully the next day in the playground, I said, 'I saw Bloody Bromley yesterday and he had a bandage on his head. Your dad must have given him a good whack.'

'He said he didn't do it,' said Sully.

Should Irish universities have ever awarded a master's degree in unique economical survival of peerless estate, Quentin Sullivan would be its first recipient, with honours, for his board always groaned with worthy comestibles, his roof never leaked, and his kin were always well shod, whether he was productively employed or not. During the course of his apprenticeship to this high estate, the long arm of the sovereign law had clobbered him from time to time as he filled his pockets with unearned income never included on tax returns. From this craft, the 'bobbies' knew him. He was also known to have whacked individuals who would place restraints upon his entrepreneurship, thus earning him some days behind bars – not the ones at the Dirty Duck Hotel. So, when Wilford Bromley, history and geography, was mashed with a big stick after caning Sullivan, Junior, Quentin Sullivan, his large dad, was hauled in as prime suspect. And he just might be guilty. With Sullivan, you never could tell.

Wilford Bromley was not enjoying domestic tranquillity when he slammed the gate of number twelve Blotchley

Crescent on Thursday morning. Mrs Bromley had incinerated his muffin, fried his eggs to a Picasso, and batted his kipper to death; his *Chipton-Downs Post* failed to arrive; and his car wouldn't start. At the 11:00 A.M. teachers' tea break, there was a cancellation because they ran out of tea. Mr Bromley, therefore, at 11:15, picked up a Paddy Lynch by the scruff of the neck and whaled several bejabbers out of him with his swishy cane.

At 4:35 P.M. on Friday, Wilford had brought his autumn day to a close and was opening the door to his Austin at the far end of the quad when a spectre parted the soft incoming mist to smack him behind the ear with a knobbly stick. Leaning over his recumbent frame, the spectre whispered in his ear, 'Don't hit the boys!'

At 5:00 A.M. Saturday, the *Chipton-Downs Post* featured a sub-leading headline, 'The Scarlet Pimpernel Strikes Again.' This was read with great exultation by all students, with howling mirth by his fellow teachers, with wrath by Bromley who threatened legal proceedings, with sobriety by Inspector Callahan, with a smile of delight by Quentin Sullivan who said he didn't do it, and with great laughter by me because I was a Kipper and sometime Kippers are like that.

It was a most delightful thwack.

'I didn't do it,' said Quentin Sullivan once again to Inspector Callahan, who said, 'Perhaps you didn't, Mr Sullivan, but you either know who did or you can find out!'

Quentin groaned.

* * *

When Sully told his mother, Sarah Sullivan, nee Considine, about Mad Harry Flanagan, his tea and chocolate eclairs, she was startled but said to her husband, Quentin, 'It's true. I knew Harry at school in Ballykenny not far from Wexford. The Flanagans now, they were a wild lot, mixed up in the Troubles with the English. Would have won medals for bravery if there had been any around and anybody to give them. I must take him some of my pea soup.'

'He's not starving, Sarah.'

'He's got lots of eclairs, Ma.'

'That's not the point. He's a foin Irish man in distress at losing the love of his life. I wonder,' she said, clutching the black shawl to herself, 'if I'll ever be missed like that.'

'Any more of those chocolate biscuits, Ma?'

'Get to bed, Francis Patrick Sullivan.'

It was the following day that she took the soup around to Turpentine Drive with her cousin, the widow Hetty McBride, who was visiting from Limerick. It seemed that they spent the entire afternoon sipping tea and talking the hours to sheer shreds. The two women had to pull their black shawls around them when they quit the cottage, for thunderous Irish clouds fresh in from Blarney were shunting overhead and the first rain was spattering the rooftops of Saint Joseph's Academy of Hard Knocks as they passed.

Mad Harry Flanagan returned the visit. It was many a year since he'd ventured from his cave in search of any new vision, or conversation with other beings in this valley of tears. The visits took root and became established. Quentin Sullivan took Harry to the Bird in Hand, where ancients cleared a space at the bar for him to polish elbows. Some Sundays later he went back to church. Everything at different speeds, you understand.

It was in February, or was it March, that civil war erupted in the teachers' common room, for Bloody Bromley had taken his cane once again to a recalcitrant student, Rich Quigley, who said that Constantinople was a football team in the Third Division. Quigley howled. He walked around the schoolyard holding his posterior and howling even hours afterwards until Francis Chumley, English teacher, questioned the cause of his distress. Rich Quigley laid it on thick. Bitter tears rolled down his cheeks like the Mersey at high tide. He wept a river.

In the common room, Chumley grabbed a furled umbrella from its stand, threatening Bloody Bromley so that a fellow teacher, Terence McNab, held Chumley's arm from striking the blow. McNab, who was from Glasgow, said, 'We should all just take Bromley outside and break his damn ribs!'

'Perhaps,' suggested Geoffrey Fisk, science, 'the Scarlet Pimpernel will strike again!'

This remark stopped everybody; it hung in the commons like a rusted guillotine or the vapours from the Dirty Duck on a Sunday morning. It was unsaid, but the question was asked: is the Scarlet Pimpernel in this common room?

The door opened and Miss Hoolihan said, 'The headmaster would like to speak to Mr Bromley immediately.'

That the Scarlet Pimpernel would strike again there was no doubt. The teaching staff knew it, the students excitedly knew it, Bloody Bromley felt it, Inspector Callahan knew it, and the editor of the *Chipton-Downs Post* knew it, but when and where? Quentin Sullivan groaned, for he knew in his Irish head that the inspector would pester him to extinction should this case not be brought to conclusion, even if it meant Quentin Sullivan revisiting old chambers. He therefore said to himself that day in March, 'There's not that much mist from the river now, but it will be when there is that the Scarlet Pimpernel will strike. I will bide until that time.'

The editor of the *Chipton-Downs Post*, Matthew Kilpatrick, held special blocks ready for printing the next sensational chapter. It was good press.

But the days crept by. Daffodils had sprung through the snow at Chipton Park like Irish blarney in the Dirty Duck. In late March, a mist formed around Quigley Head out of the bluffs, hanging low over the outer banks of the River Dee, then pushed gently inland by a friendly breeze from old Ireland. It reached the school shortly after noon and you could hear the tramp steamers sounding their melancholy horns as they slid into the gloom like the IRA after eight Guinness. 'This is it,' said Quentin

Sullivan. He took an old, bent, knobbly stick from a cupboard under the staircase, a shillelagh from the old sod. At three o'clock he put on a heavy jacket recently borrowed from Woolworth's and an old sailor hat and went to the door.

Another venturer in Chipton-Downs selected a handsome stick, the handle green and black with a well-polished brass head of a mallard duck, the tip pointed in silver. It hefted well and balanced nicely in the hand for a swing.

Bloody Bromley snapped his desk lid shut. Through the dormer window he could see shreds of mist moving in the direction of the quadrangle. He put the briefcase under his arm and clutched the car keys in his hand. Not too bad, he thought, as he headed towards his Austin, which was now parked near an exit he did not normally use, for some innate sense told him to take care – an innate sense and two clobbers from a stick. Quentin Sullivan, with a master's degree in guile and subterfuge, lurked like a thin man in a fat fog adjacent to the same exit. He saw the wisp of a figure moving, the stick fall, the groan, and the voice: 'Don't hit the boys!'

Quentin struck but missed, but he grabbed the large figure tightly about the neck. Locked in embrace, they lurched, an Irish tango in the mist, which was when Quentin saw the agitated face. 'You!' he cried.

A whistle blew across Cardington Lane; another answered it, followed by the sound of large feet running. 'Quick,' said Quentin, 'this way.' The two men slithered over the sandstone wall, through the rhododendrons, to the iron grating in the wall of the priest's house through which they scrambled, and down into a small hill of pitch-black coal.

Before the dawn crept its reluctant way up the river and melted the mist blanketing Chipton-Downs, the two figures had threaded stealthily down Pinafore Lane where a magic bottle of Irish whiskey added splendid depth to a fine pot of stolen Colombian coffee.

Sarah Sullivan said, 'Harry Flanagan, what are you and this husband of mine doing up at this unearthly hour?'

'We've been playing chess,' said Quentin, 'over at Harry's place.'

'Chess?' said she. 'You've never played chess in your Irish days. What did you steal?'

The Chipton-Downs newspaper blared, 'Scarlet Pimpernel Strikes Again!' in its next issue, adding that Mr Wilford Bromley had accepted a transfer to Harrogate Avenue School, effective immediately.

'He was sacked,' said Quentin Sullivan.

Sully absorbed the entire drama from his best listening post and told me, and I told no one. But we did visit Mad Harry Flangan and he knew that we knew, but the Irish keep these things in their hearts. The tea was made by the widow, Hetty McBride of Limerick, while Mad Harry sat with us, and you would have thought Hetty McBride had always been there, for she fitted so well at Turpentine Drive.

* * *

Inspector Callahan said, 'So you were playing chess with Mad Harry Flanagan, Mr Sullivan. I suppose he can support this checkmate?'

'Yes, Chief Inspector.'

'Not Chief yet, Mr Sullivan. Soon, perhaps.'

In the kitchen at home, my mother said to Sully and me, 'We must pray for Mr Bromley.'

And so we did.

We never saw him again.

Chapter Eleven

A Tipperary Lad

♣

'Tom Kipper, read from page seventy-one, "The Recruit".'

We were in Miss Nancy Stapleton's class at Saint Joseph's Academy of Hard Knocks, her English class, reading poetry, 'A Shropshire Lad'. She was getting shrill, full of nationalistic fervour, and full of the glory that is England. Any moment she would have us singing, 'And when they say we've always won,' and she would be dewy-eyed.

I read, 'And you will list the bugle that blows in lands of morn / And make the foes of England / Be sorry that you were born.' The headmaster, 'Pop' Devereaux, opened the classroom door and said, 'May I come in?' Pop had every school authority invested in him, and he could burn down the Education Department if he wanted to, but he exerted more discipline politely than could be exceeded by a school of professors. He was a short man, silver-haired, with enormous black eyebrows.

'Put down your pens for a moment, boys,' he said. He took a stance in front of Miss Stapleton's desk, shrugged his shoulders, and cleared his throat. 'Boys,' he said, 'I see that you are reading "A Shropshire Lad". When we read it, we feel we have a very special place in our hearts for England. As you know, the war has taken a very nasty turn and enemy forces are building up on the coast of France to invade our shores. We are very much alone against this threat to our liberty. Without giving you a big lecture, I just wanted to say this to you: should these enemy forces land on our blessed shores and ever come up here, always remember, boys, that you are Catholic and you are British, and nothing – nothing can ever take that away from you.' Muscles were twitching in his face. 'That's all, boys. Thank you, Miss Stapleton.' When he left, we were all very quiet until Miss Stapleton started crying, which was when we all started cheering for no reason at all, and it was a funny kind of day.

After school the following day, Nancy O'Donnell joined Sully and me as we picked our way through the bomb rubble to see what the park looked like after the big one dropped. There was no one around, or so it seemed, for lots of kids had been evacuated to the Lake District.

The man in front of us was a mess; all his clothes were covered in dust. We just stood there looking at him, the three of us. He looked not one bit like a German, certainly not one jot like the monsters we had been told about. The large pistol he had in his hand he dropped to the ground, just where the roundabout had been before the bomb destroyed it. He looked like one of the kids from over on Grassmere Crescent who had lost his way, wandering into enemy Catholic territory. He said, 'Hallo.'

We just stood there and said nothing.

He said, 'Ich will euch keine Angst machen.'

And we said nothing.

'Ich brauche Wasser,' he said.

Nancy O'Donnell said, 'He's asking for water, I think.' She took him by the hand and we all went with her and the big grey man to a drinking tap that was still left in the park. The man bent his head to the tap and drank like an Irishman at a wake. He rubbed his hand over his mouth. 'Das Wasser ist sehr gut.'

I was fed up with Nancy O'Donnell taking over, so I stepped forward. 'Sully and I are in command here,' I said, not believing what I was saying. He looked impressed.

'Ich glaube du willst mir etwas sagen.'

'Come with me,' I said.

All that was left of number thirty-seven Woodstock Avenue was the living room, one bedroom, the kitchen, the garden shed, one toilet, and a lot of inspiration. I motioned, and the big grey man with the blackened face, the layer of dust, the hunted look, and the wispy hair followed me like a sheep follows a shepherd.

'Glory to God!' said my mother, which was her immediate reaction to most unusual things. Apron to her mouth, she looked with Irish eyes at this large bedraggled creature from the skies. 'Where did he come from?'

'He's my prisoner. Well, mine and Sully's.'

The large grey man put his hands in the air to signify surrender. My dad, rising from his eternal armchair, said, 'Give him some tea.'

'Of course,' said my mother.

The grey man was gestured to the kitchen table, which he overwhelmed with his size. 'They're big, aren't they?' said my mother. 'Tom, tell him he can put down his arms.' I reached up and pulled his arms down.

'Danke,' he said.

No one could make tea like my mother could. The grey man was hungry, eating like Uncle Xavier's dog Grip, until he recovered composure and the hunted animal left his blue eyes. Dad's brown eyes were somewhat distressed because the guest had just eaten his rationed bacon and eggs for the week.

As he was drinking tea, his eyes caught the picture of the Sacred Heart in the gilded frame on the wall by the food cupboard. 'Sind Sie Katholisch?' he said.

We all nodded. He blessed himself. He was a lonely young man caught up in a web of circumstances, still in uniform and confused; gone were the certainty, the bravado, the songs, and the swagger. It was then that his head nodded and we all supported him to the well-worn couch in the parlour, where he crumpled in fatigue. He looked not unlike my brother Matt, in the RAF. My mother spoke to Sully and Nancy O'Donnell in a gentle but serious voice. 'The poor, wee creature is in trouble. Soon he will be in a prison camp, but we're going to look after him awhile before he has to go. Do you think we can keep it secret?'

Kids love secrets. Here was a real live one. They went home with their fingers crossed.

'I wonder what his name is,' said my mother.

The following day, a pale sun filtered through the dust and the grey man awoke to find my mother with a nice cup of tea. 'Danke,' he said.

Then it all came back to him as though it were yesterday. 'You must learn better English, Karl, in case the Spitfires get you,' said Onkel Klaus, who was the family comedian. They all laughed and raised glasses of fine Rhine wine to the Luftwaffe.

Fräulein Louise Schultz found tears in her eyes. 'You come back to me, you hear, Karl Frederickhafen.'

'Oh, I shall return, you silly Louise. I make you that promise. And now let us take a walk around the Binnen Alster and perhaps a stein at the Gasthaus.' He departed early the following morning for the Luftwaffe station, taking a train from the Bahnhof, leaving Louise with some tears in company of Onkel Klaus.

Two nights later, after briefing, the crew clambered aboard the Heinkel, with three hundred other aircraft, heading across the black North Sea to Liverpool. It was a formidable fleet. It was not a Spitfire that brought down the aircraft but flak fired randomly from a battery located near the old Roman town of Chester on the Dee. It plunged into the River Mersey along with numerous ships, only masts and funnels showing. They all bailed out, the whole crew, floating through a black night scorched red with fire of the Apocalypse. Karl Frederickhofen billowed into the playground of a park full of bomb craters, only one swing left and the public toilet in shiny red brick, where he spent the night, not sleeping. The home guard in the person of old Jack Lynch picked up the parachute in the early hours, took it back to base, and talked about it over tea and scones. 'You didn't by any chance collar the owner, did you, Mr Lynch?' asked Sergeant Logan, stirring his tea, with doubtful dispensation in his enquiry, like catching a Grimsby kipper in the Red Sea.

'I captured him, Ma,' I said, sitting down with my prisoner on the couch.

'He's probably still hungry,' fussed my mother, so we kept him like a runaway dog; we kept him the whole day while he broke out his schoolboy English; we consulted a map and decided he was from Hamburg. Sometimes he would look out of the only window that had not been broken, see the rubble, and say, 'I am sorry.'

'You speak good English,' said my mother to make him happy.

'No gute as you English,' he answered, stumbling over the words.

'Ah, we are not English,' said my mother.

He looked startled. 'Nicht Englisch?'

'No,' said my mother, pouring the tea. 'We're Irish.'

His eyes grew wider. 'Ich bin in Irland?'

I said, 'No, Karl, you are in England. But we're Irish. Isn't that right, Ma?'

'Oh, it is to be sure. More's the pity I think sometimes.'

'Is this Liverpool?' he asked.

'Aye,' Mother said. 'More or less. The capital of Ireland.'

'Ist das nicht Dublin?'

'What did you say now, Karl?' asked Mother.

'I have a brother in the RAF,' I said. 'He looks like you.'

'We should take him to Mass tomorrow,' said my mother. 'He said he's Catholic and tomorrow's Sunday.'

'Could he wear Matt's old clothes?' I asked.

'Listen here, Tom Kipper, he seems to understand you better than anybody now. See if he wants to go to Mass.'

So I talked with him. We wrote some things down on school paper, and he became delighted with the thought. Matt's clothes fitted him fairly well except for the shoes, which were cobbled for large Irish feet, but he put them on anyway. Sunday morning we walked a few short streets without rain, through some rubble strewn from the Blitz, to Saint Joseph's by Lynch Drive, next door to the Academy of Hard Knocks.

'Who's the new parishioner?' questioned Uncle Bart.

'Aye, a distant cousin of Joe's from Tipperary,' lied my mother.

'What's his name?'

'His name? What's his name, you ask. Why, it's Sean Mulcahey.'

'Good morning, Mr Mulcahey. How's old Tipperary now?' asked Bart.

Karl just looked at Bart with bloodshot eyes and said nothing.

'Doesn't understand the English yet,' said my mother, 'only the Gaelic. The pure Gaelic. And he's had the flu.'

I heard Uncle Bart mutter under his breath, 'Irish, my arse!'

We knelt in the middle of the pews on Our Lady's side, where some teenage redheaded Irish girls kept staring at Karl and smiling at each other. Katey O'Brien, the brassiest, leaned over to me and said, 'Who's the charmin' man with your mother, Tom Kipper?'

'It's me cousin from Clonmel, Sean Mulcahey,' I lied. 'Only speaks the Gaelic.'

'Aye, he looks Irish,' she smiled and went back to her friends with the hot news.

Karl was at home in the church, with the Latin, and we all went to Holy Communion. The priest, Father Ryan, gave the blessing. Outside on the church steps, the girls crowded Karl until his eyes became more bloodshot.

'A fine Irish lad,' said Mrs O'Connell, hurrying down the steps.

'Only say hello,' I whispered in his ear, but he kept saying 'Ja, ja' too many times. So we elbowed him through the crowd in the direction of home. Nancy O'Donnell and Sully followed us down Woodstock

Avenue, caught up with us at the front door, and we all tumbled into what was left of number thirty-seven. Nancy asked, 'Are you married?'

'Nein, ich bin nicht verheiratet,' he shook his head. He understood that one.

'Do you have a girlfriend?' This took some time, but he then quickly took a small photograph from an inside pocket.

'Louise,' he said, smiling a big, fat smile. Everybody took turns looking at the picture and another of his mam and dad. Then he said, 'Why you Irish in England?'

We all turned to Ma. She hesitated. 'Karl,' she said, 'Ireland is a place of the heart. It's a place we all long to be. It's a lovely green colour and the wind sings, and the people are full of laughter and sometimes, but not too much, melancholy. It has been blessed by the Lord, the Blessed Mother, and Saint Patrick. So if you are all or some of these things, then you are in Ireland, or at least you are Irish. It's where your heart longs to be. That's why we're in England but really we're in Ireland. Now can you understand that?' I always said Ma should have been an actress. Karl didn't understand. Neither did I. But don't tell anybody. That is, I didn't understand until this day and age.

'And Irishmen,' said my father from his armchair, 'are all over the world singing about it.'

'Ah, take no notice of him now,' said my mother. 'He's an Englishman.'

It was in the dark evening that the power failed again;

we lit the candles and my mother said, 'Karl, we shall have to tell the police tomorrow,' and he understood. We said the rosary together before starting to blow out the candles.

There was a knock on the front door. Before we could think of putting our guest into hiding, the door opened to Uncle Bart, bright of eye, with Lavender O'Neill, the barlady from the Bird in Hand, on his arm, and a cricket bag in his hand. But he had not taken up the game, for on the kitchen table he placed a full bottle of Red Label Scotch and a bottle of Spanish sherry. 'For the man from Tipperary, a little celebration.'

No one could produce items like that in the year of forty-one without being up to their Irish eyeballs in the black market. Clasping her bosom, my mother said, 'Where in this blessed plot did you get them from, Bart?' But Bart just poured several libations into whatever containers, glasses, and chipped cups Ma could produce.

'Sing "When Irish Eyes Are Smiling", Mary,' he said, and I could see that he had already spent some time in the Bird in Hand. Now Ma can't sing, but all Irish do anyway.

After two verses, perhaps three, Karl, red-faced and blue-eyed, after drinking three Scotches, became the loudest, most inharmonious baritone in the volunteer choir. All choir members suddenly stopped as he said, 'Venn Irish eyes are smilink, dey steal your heart av-vay.' Everybody roared. Lavender O'Neill shouted, 'You're a broth of an Irish boy!'

Ma gave me a dash of sherry in the bottom of a

chipped cup. 'Just sip it down now,' said she, starting in on an Irish jig.

'Keep the noise down,' said my dad. 'You'll wake up the home guard!'

The voices floated across the County Park, the debris, the rubble, the broken masonry of the village school, discarded cars, seashore and river, and the Irish Sea, so that should they be keen of hearing, they might have reached Eirrean's kelly green meadows themselves. Well, they might. They just might. Irish stars shone down on us.

Monday morning, Karl put on his uniform with Matt's big coat over the top and we walked through daffodils peeping up in the park to Maxwell police station.

Sergeant Keenan said, 'I wondered how long it would take you to bring him in. Looks Irish, too. From Tipperary, they say.'

Karl hugged us all, particularly my mom, and I think he cried a bit. 'Venn Irish eyes are smilink,' he said to her.

'Don't forget your beads,' she said, handing him her favourite Irish greenstone rosary.

When I bumped into Katey O'Brien in the village, she said, 'You lied to me, Tom Kipper. You'll get ten Hail Marys for that. Anyway, we're going to visit him at the camp in Wales.' She joined her friends, looking very superior as only girls can.

I said to Sully down in the dell, 'He gave me a German belt buckle. Look at this.'

Sully said, 'That's nothing, Tom Kipper. Look at this.'

And from his inside pocket he pulled out Karl's pistol. 'I went back and found it.'

So Sully bested me again.

It was only many years later that we discovered that Karl did get home to Louise to tell her he'd married a pretty Irish colleen by the name of Katey O'Brien.

Some of you may remember him. He got a job driving the number five bus from the pier head in Liverpool, driver number 46, Karl Mulcahey.

Ah then, he was a foin Tipperary lad.

Chapter Twelve

The Entwhistle
Goodhart Watch

It was at number ten, Fennel Street, southwest London, in the year 1895, that Penelope Farquar consulted the watchmaker, John Smith, personally steering him in each fine detail of the watch, of its form, although without trespass upon his superior engineering skills. Finally she requested the engraving within the back cover, for she loved Entwhistle Goodhart with all her English being. It was two months before the major went to the African colonies that she gave it to him at her parents' home in Grosvenor Square, her parents being present, for Entwhistle and Penelope were engaged, but not yet married.

Entwhistle Goodhart, Junior, became their first child after they solemnised their vows in 1896, and it was he who inherited the silver watch when his father fell for queen and country with a chest full of medals and spears.

Grandfather 'Lucky' Frank Finnegan gave me, Tom Kipper, the very same silver pocket watch, fingers delicately scrolled, surmounting an alabaster face. Attached to the case was a fob of pure silver. It was said to have been taken from the greatcoat of an English officer slain outside the Dublin post office in the losing battle of the Troubles by Padraic Finnegan, my great-grandfather, who was himself lightly injured by a stray English bullet in the closing stages of the fracas. It was a wound found worthy of many a free pint of porter when the stories were told through thick blue tobacco smoke from clay pipes or cheap Woodbine cigarettes from the enemy's country across the water.

Showed the wounds many times, did he, did Padraic Finnegan, at the request of the beaten but not vanquished. The English bullet had penetrated Great-grandpa Finnegan's gluteus maximus, and it was said that Maggie Macready, the landlady, was sick and tired of seeing the hero's big arse stuck on the bar.

'A hero is he?' she would say. 'I was the hero!'

'A foin man he was,' said my mother, words that were chiselled on his gravestone by men who knew him at the post office.

Once nestled snugly in the waistcoat pocket of Major Entwhistle Goodhart and before that his father, also major Entwhistle Goodhart, it was crafted and inscribed with living precision by J. Smith, London watchmaker.

I mentally counted the number of people who had

held it in their pockets: there was Entwhistle Goodhart Sr.; then Goodhart Jr., the son who gave his life for glory at the post office; taken by Padraic Finnegan, my great-grandfather of the wounded loins; thence to his son and heir, Lucky Frank Finnegan, my grandfather, who bypassed my mother, Mary Catherine Kipper, nee Finnegan, by giving it to me, Tom Kipper, the world's greatest time keeper. I kept it in my right-hand pants pocket, which was the only one I had without holes, taking it out from time to time to tell the world the hour. I thought I had never seen anything so perfectly made, far exceeding Big Ben, better than the clock at the Liverpool ferry or the Liver Building. That evening in the kitchen, I was holding the magic of the silver watch in my hand. It was warm from my pocket, some of the casing smooth and other parts intricately enscrolled. 'Ma,' I said, 'I wonder who Entwhistle Goodhart and Penelope Farquar were.'

'I don't suppose we'll ever know,' she said. She handwashed some English china cups and saucers. 'Doesn't it say anything in those two newspapers, the one from London and the one from Dublin? Anyway, who do you think they were?'

'Well, I think Entwhistle Goodhart was an English knight in shining armour who loved an Irish girl named Patricia Hoolihan who went over to the enemy's side and changed her name to Penelope Farquar, but she was really a spy for Ireland.'

'Heavens to Murgatroyd, child, you do have

imagination!' She put the cups on hooks, giving me that Irish look.

I went down to the dell, deep into espionage.

My good fortune was equalled by that of Uncle Bart, who escaped the clutches of Inspector Brian McCafferty by the skin of an Irish prejudice. McCafferty, with his squad of police constables, staged a raid on the illegal gambling hell at Maguire's Common. The Common was an untamed, undulating patch of ground, overgrown with weeds and thistles, stretching in haphazard fashion for a couple of miles. It was bordered by clay-bricked council houses on the west and Cherry Lane to the north; to the south lay bogs and lakes undisturbed for generations, and to the east lay Murphy's vast brewery surrounded by a wooden fence so high and so solid that we never knew anybody, man nor boy, who had ever peered over its top. Should it have been otherwise, duty-filled Irish men would be rolling English oak barrels daily.

It was on a clearing in a footpath close by this fence that the gamblers gathered, mostly Irish cloth-capped men who came together in ones and twos on Sundays, mostly wearing blue serge suits, *de rigueur*, shiny at the elbow, with collar studs but no collar or tie, just a short, white silk scarf tucked down the front of the jacket. They were 'Mick' mostly, sometimes Michael, Jack, or Sean; Coogans, Kennedys and Maguires; Hoolihans and Mahoneys.

When the raid by Inspector McCafferty and his brave PCs came, lookout men posted by Uncle Bart north and south gave the alarm and the gamblers vanished like whiskey at a wake. But it was a close call for Uncle Bart, who would never run in the Olympics unless a brewery was at the finish.

'You didn't make much of a haul, Mr McCafferty,' said his superior, Chief Inspector Longfellow. 'In point of fact, you didn't apprehend one single suspect.'

'They posted lookouts, Chief Inspector, at every point of the compass.'

'Oh, lookouts, is it? Let me remind you, Mr McCafferty, that the justices, the town council, and the magistrates all take a very dim view of illegal gambling here in the county borough. Men who have just picked up their unemployment monies have been seen heading directly toward Maguire's Common with one thought in mind: gambling. It is our job, our duty to stamp it out. If you can't catch them north or south, Mr McCafferty, then go east or west. But catch them!'

This gave McCafferty the germ of an idea that grew like a pleasant rumour. For east of the 'two-up' pitch in Maguire's Common stood the tall, imposing, pine wood fence shutting out the unwanted from Murphy's Brewery. It was from behind this barricade that McCafferty and his PCs would launch their swift and victorious assault upon the county's arch criminals. But first he must speak confidentially to the manager at Murphy's, Sean Mulcahey, a most sober individual as befitted his calling. Until after six o'clock, that is.

The plot thickened like last week's Irish stew. Then

came the day when Bart was short of a shilling. It was a warm day, and the thirst was piling up inside him, cracking his adenoids like a log in a furnace. 'Mary,' he said to my mother, rubbing his hands in great expectation, 'would you be having a shilling you could lend me?'

'Bart, I don't even have a threepenny bit.' She clutched the back of the grandpa chair with great drama. 'You know the philanthropist has decided not to work.' She nodded towards my dad asleep in the chair. 'Says by doing this he will eventually destroy Capitalism.' Tears appeared in her slate grey eyes. 'Oh, Bart, how will I manage?'

Mom, to me, was the most optimistic person in the whole universe, so the drama opening up before my very eyes had me transfixed. My three-day-old bubblegum felt as tasteless as a school lunch. Uncle Bart, too, was moved, for he and the family had always leaned heavily on Mary Catherine, his older sister, for sustenance as well as advice. Pulling the peak of his cap tighter about his Irish head, he put his arm round her shoulders and said, 'Don't worry about a thing, Mary; you will be looked after.' That very afternoon he returned to give her two pounds and ten shillings, so that my mother wept again, smothering Bart in kisses and hugs.

'But where did you find it, Bart? How did you come by such a large sum?'

'I have me friends, Mary, carefully selected.'

But we all knew that somewhere out there in the county borough, some other pilgrim in this valley of tears was minus two pounds and ten shillings, most probably more.

When 'Socks' Knell walked into the smoke through the back door of the Bird in Hand, there was a lull in the measure of conversation, for he was a tall man, as tall as a policeman, and he worked over on Maxwell Square at the police station. No one knew the exact nature of his duties, but it was known that his superior was Inspector McCafferty, and so he received nods but little conversation, for in 'The Bird', a policeman was as welcome as a bad kipper. But Bart Finnegan had a liking for Knell, measuring in him a quality of despair at his own occupation while his heart yearned for the sublime atmosphere of the gentle brogue, the parry and thrust of men with no money and a treasury of mirth.

Lavender O'Neill was on duty that night. She poured the best pint in the county, they said, and she had the sharpest tongue, albeit not the sharpest wit.

'He sent it over,' she said to Bart, putting a bottle of Guinness in front of him, 'the one from Maxwell Square.' She swabbed the bar. 'It's foin company you're keeping, Bart Finnegan.'

Bart looked across the bar at Socks Knell, who raised his glass. Bart finished his pint, picked up the Guinness, and walked around the bar. 'The back of the afternoon to you, Mr Knell. I see your team was hammered by the Reds two-nil. I thank you for the Guinness.'

'Cheers.'

Not a man or a woman in the pub looked at them as they spoke, but Finian Rafferty in the corner on the stool was all ears; Ma O'Brien, sipping shandy, sensed something was going on; and Dan Considine threw his darts but there was a great margin of error in direction.

'What,' asked Bart, wiping froth from his lips, 'is going on down at Maxwell Square?'

'Your friend, McCafferty, is on the carpet. Longfellow hung him out to dry for not apprehending one single gambling criminal. I see you're smiling.'

'Ah, it does my heart good to hear bad about McCafferty.'

'He's still on your case, you know.'

'Always will be, poor man.'

'About to strike again, he is.'

Wisps of blue smoke like cumulus drifted through the overhead lighting.

'Would you by any chance, Mr Knell, know the details?'

The two Irish heads moved closer. There was nodding and smiling and laughing and sipping at the beer. The game was afoot. 'And why,' asked Bart, gently, 'are you telling me these things, Mr Knell?'

'Because,' said Socks Knell, 'after twenty years, they're beginning to give me a pain in the arse!'

And Bart believed him, even if it did take twenty years.

The most catastrophic moment in my life was when the watch vanished.

'Where did you lose it?' asked my mother, which drove me to a frenzy.

'It was here in your sewing drawer in the console, Ma, where I always keep it.'

'That Sullivan boy was here last week; perhaps he knows where it is.'

'Sully's my best friend, Ma; he wouldn't steal it.'

'One of those Sullivans spent time in jail, they say,' said Aunt Moira from the couch.

I was absolutely forlorn. I would have lost weight by not eating if my mother had not forced quarts of Irish stew into my bony figure. At school, Sully said, 'Perhaps your ma or your pa took it.'

'Ma thought you took it,' I said, which sent Sully into a howl of laughter.

When he quieted down, he said simply, 'How could I take it? You're my best friend.'

'I know,' I answered.

Sully and I were blood brothers even though we were Irish, which, of course, precluded actually slashing our veins and tying them together. Later on in life we'd do it with Guinness.

When Inspector McCafferty and his three PCs loosened the boards in the fence after peering through the knot holes, they charged like the four horsemen of the Apocalypse upon the tightly knit group of cloth-capped men at Maguire's Common. 'You're all under arrest,' shouted McCafferty, brandishing a police stick, 'the whole lot of you!'

Not a cloth-capped man moved.

'Did you not hear what I said?' shouted McCafferty. Still no one moved. Nary a one of the red Irish faces showed alarm or fear of being pounced upon for any infraction of rule or regulation or book of statute. They looked open-mouthed and vacant-eyed at this shouting, bizarre officer of the law waving a stick.

'What appears to be the trouble, Officer?'

'Ah,' McCafferty shouted, 'Bart Finnegan! I knew the ringleader would be here. They don't call you Black Bart for nothing. This time you are all caught in the act!'

'The act of what?' asked Bart.

'Illegal gambling to start with,' said McCafferty. 'At the station there's bound to be other offences. At last I've caught you red-handed, Bart Finnegan!'

One of the PCs, Leary, was waving to McCafferty from the other side of the ring of men. McCafferty said to his closest aide, Flynn, 'What's Leary on about?'

'It's what's in their hands,' said Flynn.

'What is it?'

'I'm not sure, but I think it's rosaries.'

'Rosaries?'

'Aye, rosaries; you know, to say Hail Marys with,' said Black Bart Finnegan. 'Ah, now, Inspector, don't tell me you've forgotten your beads to the Blessed Mother.'

McCafferty looked and saw the rosaries. Every man was reverently holding a rosary.

'It's a prayer group,' smiled Bart.

'Prayer group,' ground out McCafferty through his teeth. 'You're up here gambling, which is against the law.'

'Ah, now,' answered Bart, 'how can we be gambling when we have no money? Isn't that right, my fellow Christians? Let's show the inspector we have no money.'

And every cloth-capped man turned his pockets inside out. It was then that they started laughing. Even the police constables joined in.

'Would the inspector,' asked Black Bart, 'care to join us in the glorious mysteries we are just about to start?' He extended a rosary. The howls of laughter started again.

When McCafferty was demoted to PC for one year after the incident, he was given a beat near the village market. A change seemed to come over him. He laughed more and they say he never missed a chance to say a rosary. I passed him on Flint Street when Sully came running up to me. 'Hey, Tom,' he said, 'I've seen your watch!'

'You what?'

'I've seen your silver watch.'

'Where, where is it?'

'It's in Cohan's.'

'What? Cohan's? How can it be in Cohan's?'

'I went inside and saw it.'

'How did you go inside? Kids aren't allowed in Cohan's.'

'Well, I saw Mrs Duffy about to go in. There were some other women with her. They were going in to pawn something or to redeem something. Me ma said they do it every week. So I slipped inside with them.'

'But how do you know it's my watch?'

'I've seen you with it hundreds of times. It was on a shelf behind the counter where Mrs Duffy said Cohan puts stuff to be redeemed.'

'Redeemed?'

'That means people who own them come to get them back.'

'But it's mine! How did it get in Cohan's?'

'Come on,' said Sully. 'Let's go along there anyway.'

We walked up the lane near the school, past Coogan's Corner, and along Lynch Drive. Cohan was too preoccupied to see two spotty Irish faces, noses to the window, looking at him. I couldn't see the watch from the window.

'I'm going in,' I said.

'He'll kill you,' said Sully.

'I'm going in.'

The bell over the door rang. The store was empty except for Cohan.

'Vot you boys doing in here? Get out!'

'Mr Cohan, can I speak to you?'

'Get out immediately!'

'I want to buy a watch.'

Cohan stopped. 'You, a little boy, vant to buy a vatch?'

'Yes, Mr Cohan.'

'And vich vatch, may I ask, do you vant to buy?'

'That one on the shelf.'

'That one?'

'Yes, the silver one.'

'That's a valuable vatch. Besides, it is not for sale. You have money?'

'Yes,' I lied.

'He got a lot of money for his birthday from a rich uncle in Australia,' lied Sully.

I swallowed hard. Sully lied better than I did.

'It's not for sale,' said Cohan. 'Maybe next week if the man does not redeem it this afternoon.'

'Can we come back?'

Cohan pondered this. 'OK,' he said. 'The man is coming at three o'clock this afternoon. If he does not come, then you come back with your momma or your poppa and I vill sell it to you. Now, please get out of my shop!'

We slammed the door behind us.

Across the other side of Lynch Drive was an acacia tree outside Mickey's Fish Market. 'Let's hide behind that tree,' I said, 'and wait to see who comes to get my watch.'

'It's only twelve o'clock,' said Sully. 'Let's go over to Mahoney's and steal some apples; then we'll come back.'

We passed Father Maguire on the way and saluted him. Sully said, 'He's the best priest to go to confession to; he knows all the players in the Liverpool football team. Says Liverpool is the capital of Ireland.'

'So does Uncle Bart.'

We were behind the acacia tree in plenty of time before three o'clock to unravel the mystery of the missing silver watch. 'Here comes Margaret Donovan,' said Sully.

'Ignore her and she might vanish.'

Margaret Donovan was the tidiest girl I ever knew. Her black patent-leather shoes always shone and her white stockings never fell down. Her superior face shone like a rosy pippin, her golden pigtails were dancing, and her horn-rimmed glasses were neatly atop her tiny nose.

'She's going to talk to us,' I said to Sully.

'Ugh, nothing makes me so sick.'

Margaret Donovan said, 'You boys are up to no good.'

'Did you hear a dog barking?' asked Sully.

'I'm going to tell Police Constable McCafferty about you.'

'Tell him we're robbing the Bank of England, Margaret,' I said.

'Try being polite, Tom Kipper!' She stood there, feet astride, hands on hips, mouth parted, looking for a good verbal duel, which she usually won.

Sully, past master in the art of insult, said, 'Margaret, if you had another brain, it'd be lonely.'

That did it. She stomped off, black plastic bag swinging, down Lynch Drive, just as I saw Uncle Bart walk along the opposite sidewalk and into Cohan's. We slipped across the street like phantom spirits to peer through Cohan's window. Bart's back was to us as he leaned on the glass counter while Cohan took the watch from the shelf and exchanged it for a white bill from Bart's hand. 'It's a five-pound note,' said Sully. 'My dad owned one once, I think.'

We scrambled back from the doorway as Uncle Bart came out. He didn't see us at first, but when he did he stopped, looked at me, looked at the watch in his hand, smacked his lips, adjusted the peak of his cap, handed the watch to me, and said, 'Tom Kipper, I was going to make this a surprise. I discovered the thief who stole your watch. I made him give me the money to redeem it. I fought him tooth and nail, I did. That's how I got this black eye. But now your watch is back.'

I found tears in my eyes. 'Thank you, Uncle Bart.' His hand was on my shoulder, and I found myself putting my arm round him. There was no one greater than my Uncle Bart.

'What was the name of the man who stole it?' asked Sully.

'What was that?'

'Who stole the watch?'

Bart looked at Sully. He took off his hat, put it back on again, and very deliberately said, 'It was a villain named Sean Mulcahey, lad. Now I must be on my way.' And off he strode down Lynch Drive.

'He's lying,' said Sully.

'Don't you say that about my Uncle Bart!'

'He's lying, I tell you. I can tell when a person's lying.'

'He gave me back my watch, didn't he?'

'Yes, but . . .'

'Then he can't be lying. Why should he lie?'

'I can prove it.'

'How?'

'He didn't have a black eye.'

The following week I waited until one day when my mother was alone in the kitchen peeling scroungy-looking Irish potatoes.

'Ma,' I asked, 'does Uncle Bart tell lies?'

'How could you say – let alone think – such a thing, child? Why, he's the very salt of the earth. What would I have done without the two pounds, ten shillings he gave me when we didn't have a sixpence and all your father did was destroy the Capitalist system in that grandfather's chair without moving a muscle? No, a lie would never, ever pass his saintly lips. You heard, of course, about that policeman, McCafferty, trying to break up his prayer group on the common. I don't know how that got into your head, Thomas Kipper!'

'When he got my watch back for me from Cohan's, where did he get the money?'

'Ah, that's a good tale. The manager of the brewery, Sean Mulcahey, gave Bart ten pounds when he was told about McCafferty trying to stop the men from praying.' She wiped her hands on her apron. A light illuminated her eyes. 'Mr Mulcahey once proposed to me when I was very young.'

'You mean he wanted to marry you?'

'That was his intention.'

'But you married Dad.'

'Your father won my heart with his English blarney.'

'I'm glad, Ma.'

'So am I,' she said, smiling her Irish smile.

I wandered down to the dell.

I looked at the watch. I wondered what Entwhistle Goodhart thought about all this and his lady love, the Irish spy, Penelope Farquar.

So, Uncle Bart said he got the money from Sean Mulcahey and Ma said so, too.

For once Sullivan was wrong.

And when I come to think of it in my Irish heart of hearts, Uncle Bart did have a black eye, too.

I wonder what the other fellow looked like.

Chapter Thirteen

The Revenge of Lavender O'Connor

Schoolyards are where heroes, saints, and sinners are made. You were mashed together, shaken down, and sieved out until you emerged gasping, full of maths, Catholicity, and yards of essays – a whippersnapper on the streets. You became a plumber, a priest, a nun, or a good-for-nothing.

'Ma,' I said, 'I think I want to be a plumber.'

'Have you spoken to your father about it?'

'No, not yet, but I will. Hey, Dad, what do you think: I think I want to be a plumber.'

'The Capitalist system,' he answered, 'is doomed.'

'What about plumbers, Dad?'

'Marx and Lenin said so.'

But Dad was fixed on saving the world with his

Dreaded Dogma Football Team, who told him all things. When they got into power, they killed off all the kings, queens, and aristocracy, sharing the wealth. They took to the game like black widows. Then they killed each other. They were very good at it. It was a very merry massacre.

Have you ever been in an empty schoolroom, an empty schoolyard, where ghosts linger; it's a haunting melody. I'd leave it empty when I became a plumber.

'He's not listening to me, Ma.'

'Why don't you ask him tomorrow when he's playing at home.'

'Hey, Ma.'

'What is it?'

'The O'Connors are being chucked out of their house. Can't pay the rent. Can Mickey O'Connor come and live with us?'

'Don't be silly, child. We haven't room to swing a cat.' She paused a moment. 'Why don't you ask your father. His friend, Karl Marx, said we will share all things in common. Perhaps he's got a double bed in the Kremlin.' She dashed an iron over faded blue undershorts. 'Unless it's occupied by a comrade-in-arms.' She chuckled over this, bashing the iron on the ancient shorts.

The Dirty Duck was just around the corner from Saint Joseph's Academy of Hard Knocks, not far down Birch Street, set back from the pavement to accommodate two large birch trees for late habitués of the Dirty Duck to lean against after accommodating an extra measure of fine ales, Gordon's gin for the ladies.

In the long history of alehouses, worthy names had been bestowed upon them such as the King's Head, the Coach and Horses, Fox and Hounds, and even the Nag's Head – illustrious names. But the very first proprietor, Charlie Higgins, who built the inn in 1726, wanted it called the Dirty Duck, and so it became. They say he actually cried in his beer when the builders erected the gilded sign and watered the first birch trees with a quart of nut brown ale. The half timbering on the exterior has bent and mellowed with age, very much like the inhabitants. Uncle Bart, of course, was one of them.

And he was the one who knew Brinsley O'Connor – he practically wrote his biography, for Bart was a biographer extraordinaire after a quart of good Guinness straight from the tap.

Foley's Scrap Iron yard was a delight to the eyes and ears of Mickey O'Connor and me, Tom Kipper. Kids weren't allowed in the yard unless they were helping their dads to cart in iron, steel, lead, and alloys of dubious cast, ninety per cent stolen, new and hammered into antiquity by cloth-capped men, sharp of face, Paddy-pig-Irish, with muffler around the neck (*de rigueur*) and red hair.

'Ah, now, where did you get that rubbish from?' Foley would ask, poking with his boot at an unbagged bunch of springs and wires. 'Did yeh smash up yer own bed or somebody else's?'

'There's some good stuff there, Mr Foley, now. Pure

Sheffield steel the lot of it.' So would say Bart Finnegan, whose hand had debagged the rubbish but whose heart was into a pint of Guinness at the Bird in Hand.

Foley would heave an ancient sigh, purse his lips, rock from one foot to the other, and then give him one and six. Finnegan would look at the coins on the palm of his Irish hand, blink his Connemara blue eyes, and head for the Bird. Better keep a shillin' for the missus.

Mickey O'Connor and I always went to Foley's with his dad, Brinsley O'Connor, or my Granddad Finnegan. They were big men at Foley's, bringing to his emporium first-grade metals obtained nocturnally when decent citizens were wrapped in the arms of Morpheus or Guinness.

Lavender O'Connor, Brinsley's missus, was a cleaning lady of sorts. I could just not imagine her taking revenge on somebody, for whenever I went home from school with Mickey, who was in the same class, he would sometimes take me home with him first, down Petticoat Lane, which should have been called Smelly Lane, and his mother, Lavender, would always give me a huge cup of tea and a digestive biscuit. It wasn't really a cup; it was a mug with a picture of King George the Fifth or Sixth, drowning in medals they won at Buckingham Palace, on one side, and the Union Jack on the other.

She would always ask me about my mother. When I got home, I would tell my mother this, and she seemed uncomfortable with the knowledge. As she peeled away at glistening white spuds, she would mutter, 'She's got two sides to her, that woman,' which was as indigestible to me as the wet, dark-green cabbage inflicted upon my anaemic Irish body twice a week – at least.

It was Mickey who told me. He also swore me to binding secrecy upon pain of death by a push off the Liver Building. 'She said she's gonna get the bitch,' said Mickey. 'She's not going to murder her or anything like that because that would be too good for her. No, she's going to take something she really loves – her house – and burn it to the ground.' I felt a vicarious thrill when he said that because I had been reading *The Man in the Iron Mask*, who exacted revenge by putting his enemy in the same iron mask. I think his enemy was his ugly brother, and although my elder brother, Matt, was a constant pain in the gluteus maximus, I would not deck him in a heavy mask; I would sooner tie him to a mad dog. Well, I might forgo that torture for, say, a shilling bribe.

'Me ma,' said Mickey, 'took a whole day to clean Mrs Trotter's house on the Hill. It's up on Glenfax Drive where the millionaires live. When she was finished, Mrs Trotter paid me ma off with a half-crown and a sixpence. Ma said she should have received two half-crowns, but the woman shut the door in her face.'

'When is she going to take revenge?'

'Don't know.'

'If you can find out, we can watch it.'

'She'll never tell.'

'I don't think your mother would do a thing like that.'

'Just you wait and see, Tom Kipper.'

'Wanna go over to Foster's and steal some apples?'

*   *   *

Bunter McCabe was the biggest kid in our school, perhaps the world. His legs seemed to swell outside his shorts like Mr Finnegan's pork sausages down at the market that were fifty per cent breadcrumbs, according to Aunt Madge. Sometimes we'd call Bunter McCabe 'Piggy', and he once said, 'Next person who says that I'm gonna kill!' Justice was measured thus at Saint Joseph's Academy of Hard Knocks.

Miss Harriet Pilkins had a very shrill voice, very English, warbling her vowels as she took us in religious studies. 'Now, class, today we will dispense with our penny catechisms – even though it is surely an indispensable tool – and discuss instead any moral subject of your choosing.' She wiped the blackboard free of chalk.

'She's crackers,' whispered O'Connor.

'At your age, you must be bursting with questions to which you are just bursting to know the answers. Remember, next year you will be saying farewell to Saint Joseph's to head out into a perhaps cruel world. Now, who is first?'

Eileen Lanahan asked coyly about becoming a nun, so Patrick ('Spits') Doyle asked about becoming a monk in a cave in the Himalayas without any knowledge about how Liverpool and Everton were doing in the First Division. Sean Flanagan asked what happened if you told a big, whopping lie in the confessional.

Miss Pilkins answered all of these questions and even asked us what we thought. Then she said, 'Tom Kipper, don't you have a question to ask?'

I had chosen a seat three-quarters of the way back in the classroom to hide behind 'Piggy' McCabe. I thought this made me invisible. It seemed that all the girls, who always sat in the front benches, swivelled their eight hundred sneering eyes on me, who just wanted to be left alone in the twilight zone.

'Revenge,' I said. I didn't really say it. It jack-in-the-boxed out like the spirit of a dog with fleas. I put my hand over my impetuous mouth, but it was too late.

'Very interesting and very original, Tom Kipper,' exclaimed Miss Harriet Pilkins.

Eight hundred eyes glowed lovingly at Tom Kipper.

'Now, Tom, why did you introduce the subject, eh, why?'

'*The Man in the Iron Mask*,' I said.

'Ah, ha, Alexandre Dumas.'

'Yes,' I said. 'He got his just revenge.'

Miss Pilkins tapped the chalk on her desk. Particles of white dust glittered in the lone sunbeam filtering through the schoolyard window. 'Tom, there is no such thing as just revenge. No revenge is just. Revenge is just a cruel emotion human beings must suppress. It is written in scripture, "Revenge is mine, sayeth the Lord." '

Eight hundred girls' eyes said, 'Didn't you know that, Tom Kipper!'

I was dazed, mortified, squished, pulverised. 'But,' I protested, 'he was just getting his own back!'

'Which is a sin,' said Miss Pilkins.

I couldn't understand that.

Neither could Sean Maloney, Conks Murphy, Whacker Doyle, or Fred Magee. We exacted revenge daily.

It didn't stop there.

'If you are stricken,' said Miss Pilkins, 'you must turn the other cheek. It is written in the Bible. Our Lord said so. If we wish to eventually arrive in heaven, we must obey these commands.'

'Oh, shit!' said Whacker Doyle under his breath.

The bell rang.

'Class is over,' said Harriet Pilkins.

Boys hastened to the schoolyard to exact revenge. Not on girls, though. You never hit a girl. It was the unwritten law of Saint Joseph's Academy of Hard Knocks. You could never, ever smack a girl in the kisser. And that wasn't in the Bible.

How could you not take revenge? It was sweet.

When I went through the cloakroom and emerged into the undecided English sunlight of the schoolyard, I was so immersed in Miss Pilkins's exhortation to never take revenge that at first I didn't notice the shadow excluding what was left of the sunshine (so that it was almost twilight). Suddenly I realised the gigantic shadow had been engendered by none other than 'Piggy' McCabe. I knew I was doomed from the start. Alicia McGivens, who loved me dearly, shouted, 'Look out, Tom Kipper!' but it was too late; the blade of the guillotine fell and I found my body clinging to the sandstone of the church library with a choir of Piggy McCabes grunting in my ear: 'You called me Piggy. Now you can take your just revenge, Kipper! Ha, ha, ha, ha,' not more than ten thousand times, like the Vatican choir gone slightly bonkers.

'No,' said Big Hughie Finnegan, my overgrown cousin, 'I'll take it for him!' He hovered over Piggy McCabe like the knell of doom and smiled at him. Before Piggy could even evade his grasp, Big Hughie dug his clenched fist into Piggy's stomach. The audience of good Catholic boys said, 'Aaaahh,' in unison and in admiration as the victim clutched his solar plexus and sank gasping to the schoolyard like a Grimsby kipper. It was a slaughter.

But I never took my revenge. I felt uncertain about whether I should take it anyway. Miss Pilkins's voice still rang in my ears, 'Revenge is mine, sayeth the Lord.'

But Ma was right – there were two sides to Lavender O'Connor: the one we knew down Stinky Lane who with the bright smile and the large mugs of steaming tea won my heart; and the other, the charlady with the slickest pair of carbolic hands that had ever shuffled a deck of cards.

Mrs Bright-Chalmondeley was seated in her library around a highly polished card table with Mrs Garrison-Smythe and Miss Emily Barrington-Jones at ten o'clock one Tuesday morning in May. A tired English sun was pushing itself through scuddy, ragged clouds over the Irish Sea when she, Mrs Bright-Chalmondeley, said, 'Margaret wasn't able to come over again, my dears, so we're one short for the game.'

'What is wrong with the poor dear?' enquired Mrs

Garrison-Smythe, smiling. 'Is she adding to the family again, is she?'

'Well, she is Catholic, you know, my dear,' said Miss Emily Barrington-Jones, smiling back, reshaping the cards in her hand.

Mrs Bright-Chalmondeley said, 'Girls, we need a fourth,' which by the strangest of circumstances was when Lavender O'Connor walked into the room with her mop and pail and a bright red bandanna holding in embrace her black sheen of hair, she of the black Irish.

It was almost as though Lavender said, 'I'm a fourth.' Lavinia Bright-Chalmondeley said, 'Do you have any money?' and Lavender answered, 'Only the five bob you're going to pay me today.' And that's how it all happened.

'We're playing poker,' said Lavinia.

'I love poker,' said Lavender. 'I hate bridge.'

The ladies all lost graciously and with much charm to Lavender O'Connor with whom they all fell overwhelmingly in love. When the game expired at thirty minutes past the noon hour, she moved expeditiously with the mop and pail to complete her housekeeping duties as ladies furnished her with half-crowns, shillings, and sixpences, Mrs Betty Garrison-Smythe twittering, 'It's my house next Thursday, Mrs O'Connor. Don't forget.' Nobody but nobody called her Lavender because of her class calling and the fact that when she lost a hand she used strange-sounding, Anglo-Saxon expletives, such as 'Oh, shit!'

Lavender kept a pot at home buried deep in her

personal underthings in a bureau drawer, into which she deposited at most regular intervals handfuls of British silver coins wrapped in pound notes. Until Miss Stapleton, that is, down at the chandlery, showed her how to open an account at the Bank of England, which loved charladies with money. The account grew recklessly.

All the ladies on the Hill came to know Lavender O'Connor, even Mrs Trotter, the one whose house Lavender said she would one day burn to the ground. Mrs Trotter seethed. She would not, or could not, invite Lavender to her home on the Hill after depreciating her labour by two shillings; thus, the Hill crowd rarely enjoyed her doubtful company at Trotter Villas. So she missed the ladies and the dirt.

'What the devil's wrong with you, Margo?' asked Chester Trotter, brushing a cat hair from his sleeve. 'It's that damn cat, isn't it? I told you to stop giving it tea.'

'No, no,' ground out Margo. 'It's that snotty char-woman, O'Connor.'

'Get rid of her,' said Chester Trotter. 'There's a war on!'

'Sell lots of insurance, darling,' said Margo, handing him his black felt hat.

'I have people to do that,' said Chester Trotter briskly.

Barrington, the chauffeur, saluted him into the Rolls.

'Remember that old piece of ground down on Bailey Street, not far from Mariner's Wharf?' asked Lavender of Brinsley.

'Aye, I do, lass.'

'Foley could use that for his scrap.'

'And why should you, me darling, be interested in Foley's scrap?'

Lavender whisked the eggs into a scramble. 'Brinsley, me pet, it's you I'm thinking of.'

'Me?'

She drew a dining chair close to him. 'You could own that plot of ground and be in the scrap business. Everywhere in the country they're tearing down iron railings and crying out for metal for the war effort. Bailey Street is close by to ship and train.'

'Where on earth, woman, would I get the money to buy the Bailey lot?'

Lavender whisked the eggs furiously. 'I've got it,' she said.

It was thus and so that Brinsley O'Connor, purveyor of ancient scrap metals of many shapes and sizes and bits, bought a parcel of ground on Bailey Common, comfortably adjacent to sundry transportation. Brinsley ('Old Scrap Iron') O'Connor was in the throes of legend.

'All I need now is a lorry,' he said.

'It's coming soon,' answered Lavender. 'Soon, my sweet.'

Two more cleaning jobs on the Hill, and she had it.

Mrs Betty Garrison-Smythe had the chauffeur, Binkley, drive it over the bridge to aroma-filled Bailey Street.

'How will I get back to the Hill?' asked Binkley.

Brinsley said, 'I'll drive you back in me new lorry.' And

he did, smiling all the way, stopping once on the way back to admire Millionaire's Row. He parked the lorry to listen to the sound of leaves falling and the expensive silence, the spacious front lawns, three-storey-high Georgian houses, and money building in the bank like scrap iron in his yard. He let in the clutch and went down to the Dirty Duck.

Mrs Betty Garrison-Smythe said to Lavender, 'Arthur has wanted to get rid of that lorry for a long time, my dear.' Taking Lavender's arm she continued, 'Now don't forget next Thursday.'

'Mickey O'Connor's ma paid the rent, Ma, so he doesn't need to come and live here.'

'Is that right, Thomas Kipper? And how do you know all these things?'

'They're getting rich.'

'Rich?' My mother stopped folding the laundry and her eyes beaded on me like a spider on a caterpillar lunch.

'They've all got new shoes.'

'That makes them rich?'

'Well, there's a lot of other things: new curtains, a tablecloth with big squares in it, and a copper teakettle.'

'Aye, I knew there was something going on with that Lavender O'Connor. She hasn't been to the Women's Guild and I haven't seen her down at the village in ages.'

'That's because she's up on the Hill playing cards.'

I thought me ma was going to have a fit. 'What on earth are you talking about, boy?'

'Well, Miss Stapleton down at the chandlery had me

169

take up some firewood and turpentine and some other things to Mrs Garrison-Smythe at Wycliffe Drive up on the Hill, and Mrs O'Connor was there playing cards with Mrs Smythe and two other posh ladies in their parlour.'

'They let you go into the parlour?'

'No, you see, the back door was open and I couldn't get an answer, so I went in and ended up in the parlour.'

'Lavender O'Connor was playing cards with them?'

'Yes, and I think she was winning all the money.'

'Holy cow!'

'So anyway, she paid the rent and Mickey doesn't have to stay with us.'

My mother smoothed out a piece of linen that was already flatter than one of Aunt Moira's infamous pancakes. 'Will you be going back there again?'

'Well, Miss Stapleton has quite a few customers on the Hill now, so I suppose I will.'

I was a purveyor of news. Good, gossipy news. Everybody loves news – good, bad, or freshly ground from the mill. But gossipy news fires the heart and titillates the ego, and it is succulent and tasty. It's almost as exciting as revenge. And me ma needed my news.

Brinsley O'Connor, scrap merchant extraordinaire, prospered like Irish blarney in manure. A patron of the Dirty Duck, peon of the old country, he was now awarded a turning sea of heads as he fanned his way through blue Woodbine smoke from the front door.

Brinsley had never been in 'the lounge' – that was occupied mostly by shopkeepers, the merchant class, men who clinked half-crowns in their pockets, smoothed out crinkled pound notes, and smoked nut-brown pipes.

Brinsley O'Connor was now a king of Ireland in the bar, in the honest pub, the good old Dirty Duck. Every man in the world experiences fifteen minutes of glory. But not Brinsley. And here, in the sanctuary of the Dirty Duck, were the men who brought him copper, brass, and pig iron of dubious origin and quality, which he in turn turned over to His Majesty's war industry at most enormous gratuity. He became rich overnight.

The Dirty Duck never had it so good.

'There's going to be a raid tonight,' said Abigail Murphy, sipping her Guinness with great relish.

'Perhaps we should all go back to the ould country,' said Bridey Catchpole.

'You're already in the ould country,' said Abigail. 'You're English.'

'Me mother,' said Bridey, 'was a Sullivan out of Waterford and proud of it. Was never once late for Mass.' She sipped from her glass of ale. 'How do you know there's going to be a raid? After the Blitz in May, it was all over. The Germans are bombing London. It must be lovely on the Liffey right now.'

At ten thousand feet, Heinrich Schultz, bombardier, said to his pilot, Herman Grossenheimer, 'How can we identify Liverpool with all this stratus?'

'It will be easy, Heinrich – Liverpool will be burning from end to end.'

'That was last May. Tonight there are just two hundred of us.'

'Just drop the bombs when I say, Heinrich. Maybe, just maybe, there will be time for a drop of Schnapps when we return. The Führer is speaking tonight.'

Chance is an elusive commodity.

Chance took the Heinkel carrying Heinrich and Herman to Merseyside, where levers were pressed to release heavy explosive devices and incendiaries to sink ferry boats and oil tankers, but some of them missed because the bombardier could hardly wait to return to the Fatherland for his Schnapps.

One of the bombs struck the cricket club at Fair Meadows, where the president, a Mr Vincent Farquart, made a speech the following weekend under canvas, condemning all Hun barbarians between draughts of Gordon's gin.

He particularly condemned their grossly inept marksmanship: 'They could have at least dropped them in the Mersey,' he said. Two or three incendiaries struck the Hill, all in one selected spot, a most elegant Georgian mansion doing nothing but minding its own business. It was not burned to the ground; fifty per cent survived, which was large by Saint Joseph's Academy of Hard Knocks standards, but treacherous, beyond all imaginings, impossible to live with, out of the question by its owner's, who emerged from her private air raid shelter at the 'All Clear' without lipstick.

* * *

Brinsley O'Connor couldn't put a foot wrong. Patrons of Foley's slipped by his ancient yard like Irish traitors down to Brinsley's Scrap, where they acquired a penny a pound more for their bags of trash and a free pint every time Brinsley set his Irish foot through the front door, cleaved through the Woodbine stratus of Ye Olde Dirty Duck, and bellied up to the bar. He even treated Tom Foley to a pint of lager. 'You've done well, matey,' said Foley. 'I was growing tired of collecting junk anyway. Do you know I've bought and sold Mrs Lavery's washing machine three times. Let me know if you want any more garbage.' The Prince of Wales never had it so good. It was as though Brinsley's offspring, Mickey and Sissy, were of much larger dimension at 15 Petticoat Lane on fish and chips and Texas potatoes arriving from America, in addition to which Mrs Lavender O'Connor needed more room for additional wardrobe from Marks and Spencer.

With the most splendid light that only inspiration can engender, Brinsley deserted his battered apple box desk in the shed on Bailey Common and growled his red lorry at some speed west along the boulevard and up to Wycliffe Drive on the Hill. There were four Estate Agent signs hanging on the drive, four of them, more than there had ever been.

'I could not possibly take that price for the property, Mr O'Connor. Why, it's already listed much below standard.'

173

'Ferguson, the owner's, down in Australia,' said Brinsley, 'singing "God Save the King" to the Abos. He'll take ten bob for this lot.'

'I'll think about it,' said Bradley Jones.

'I'll wait,' said Brinsley.

Bradley Jones licked his lower lip and mopped his brow after first removing his trilby hat. 'Let's have a drink and talk it over.'

'Down at the Dirty Duck,' said Brinsley O'Connor.

'The Dirty Duck?'

'Me favourite pub. Around the corner from Saint Joseph's.'

'Let's go to my club,' said Bradley Jones. 'It's just around the corner by the county library.'

'Me luv,' said Brinsley O'Connor to his wife, Lavender, when he drove home in his red lorry, 'we're movin'.'

'Moving?'

'Up the Hill, me darling.'

'The Hill?'

'Seventy-two Wycliffe Drive. And guess who lives across the street.'

'Eh?'

'Your old friend, Margo Trotter.'

Lavender dropped the frying pan with a great clang. For once her vocal cords were held in ultimate quiescence; she shut up and followed Brinsley into the red scrap-iron lorry up the Hill to gawp, slack-jawed, at her new home, Fotherington Manor.

'The windows need cleaning,' she said, and Brinsley

O'Connor laughed all the way down to the Dirty Duck.

* * *

There were six of us sitting on the laundry wall: Sean Maloney, Conks Murphy, Whacker Doyle, Fred Magee, Gobs Flanagan, and me, Tom Kipper. We didn't move until Mrs McCaffrey told us to do so with a broom.

'It was in the news,' said Whacker Doyle.

'Me dad,' said Conks Murphy, 'said a ferry boat was sunk, the Liver Building was hit, the post office, the Guinness Brewery, the *Liverpool Echo*, and the Dirty Duck.'

'Your dad,' said Gobs Flanagan, 'is daft!'

'Me ma said they bombed a house on the Hill,' volunteered Whacker Doyle. 'I hope it wasn't Mickey O'Connor's. And if they bombed the Guinness Brewery, they'd have to go to Ireland.'

'Maybe they've declared war on Ireland,' said Conks.

I said, 'They wouldn't dare. Anyway, let's go and see if Mickey O'Connor is OK on the Hill. Anybody wanna go up there?'

It was a good stretch of the Irish legs, five Irish miles, avoiding suspicious-looking policemen on the way, always asking where we were going as though we were Nazi espionage agents. Next time I'll tell them Berlin. We went through Forsyth Park and along the Promenade, playing tag along the way, but I found my thoughts were of Mickey and Mrs Lavender O'Connor and where the bombs had dropped.

There was no school that day because of the air raid, which meant that we kids had an excellent opportunity to get out there and steal something not securely fastened down.

The Dirty Duck, which we had passed en route, was in good shape, smelling of vinegary, stale beer and Woodbines, so we knew that Conk Murphy's dad really was daft. 'Hard Knocks' was OK, too, with not one person in the schoolyard.

A short distance from the Hill, we passed through shopping area streets that were far superior to our village, and the accents of the women shoppers seemed to engage them in shrill conflict with each other.

'They're all crackers,' said Flanagan.

'Wycliffe Drive,' twittered one of them in a dense gossipy pool, 'went up in smoke last night.'

We all heard her voice at the same time.

'Go and ask her,' said Fred Magee.

'Excuse me, miss,' I said to the twittering lady, 'where is Wycliffe Drive?'

'Why, it's up there, young man, where the smoke is. Do you boys live around here?'

Up and over the rooftops and trees we could see a wisp of blackish smoke trailing out towards the Irish Sea. So we ignored the twittering lady and started to move faster, quickening our sluggish steps, and broke into a canter.

At the bottom of the drive, we saw a lone red fire engine and two men rolling up hoses, stamping feet, and taking off hats, and we knew that the fire was probably over. At the big iron gates we saw half a Georgian house, one side crisp as a cinder, black rubble on the green lawn, and an ancient oak black on one side but standing.

'Mickey O'Connor's probably gone,' said Sean Maloney.

'Don't be daft,' said Whacker Doyle. 'There he is over there.'

Mickey O'Connor came running towards us breathlessly but whooping like mad. 'Hey, lads, what are you doing here?'

'We thought you'd died and gone to heaven,' said Whacker.

'Sorry about your smashing house, Mickey,' I said.

He looked at me and then broke into laughter. 'This is not our house, stupo. Our house is across the street. It's called Fotherington Manor.'

'Oh,' I said. 'Then who does this house belong to?'

'Mrs Margo Trotter and all the Trotters.' He stopped and looked at me with great mischief. 'I told you me ma would get her revenge!'

You could have knocked me down with the *Liverpool Echo*, late edition, wet on the doorstep. 'I don't believe you,' I stuttered out.

He laughed again. 'I'm kidding you, Tom. In fact, me ma took pity on the Trotters, and they're living at our house until they can go and live with a cousin of hers in Llangollen.'

'Your mother forgave Mrs Trotter?'

'Yes, honest. Hey, come on, gang, over to the house.'

'Why don't you kids clear off,' shouted a fireman.

'Why don't you shut up,' shouted back Gobs Flanagan, and we all ran across the street.

Lavender made a large pot of tea and buttered delicious scones for seven boys who were forever starving. The house overwhelmed and delighted us. 'The Trotters are resting upstairs,' she said. 'They didn't get much sleep last night.'

Lavender gave me an extra buttered scone; I felt she loved me as part of the family. I also felt a certain empathy with her because she never got her revenge and neither did I. 'Would you like another cup of tea, Tom?' she asked.

And just for the record, according to Uncle Bart Finnegan, biographer extraordinaire, Brinsley ('Old Scrap Iron') O'Connor and his wife, Lavender, at the following Sunday ten o'clock Mass at Saint Joseph's Catholic Church (round the corner from the Dirty Duck), placed a large, white, crisp five-pound note on the second collection plate . . .

for the poor people down Smelly Lane.

Chapter Fourteen

Finder's Keepers

♣

'Well, it's almost true, Ma,' I said, 'isn't it?'

If you allow your imagination free rein, your creative intelligence to run riot, anything – even your common sense – can be 'almost true'. Why think any other way? Why let hard facts hinder your socks-to-your-ankles journey when you're thirteen?

The motherly hand, famous for stirring up the finest pot of Irish stew in the whole of northwest England, pulled my left ear out of its normal shape. 'No, it's not!' she emphasised. 'It is either true or it is not true. There are no in-betweens. There is a great distinction between black and white. What do they teach you at that school?' She let go of my ear to allow my head to shrink to normal size. I moved out of range of the great Irish stew hand.

'Black and white,' I said, holding my ear, 'could be mixed together to grey!' And then I fled.

'You come back here, Tom Kipper,' I heard her shout, knowing, of course, I wouldn't and that I was heading to Kirby Park to look for Paddy Sullivan.

'What did she say?' asked Sullivan.

'I said we didn't really start the fight, that we were provoked.'

'Hey, good word, provoked.'

'Mrs Shaunnassey told her that we hit them first.'

'You hit them first, not me.'

'Well, we were provoked.'

'Yeah. Provoked.'

'I told her that was almost true and she went batty.'

'Me ma goes batty, too.'

'What did you tell your ma?' asked Tom Kipper.

'Nothing – I told me dad.'

'What did he say?'

'He laughed his bloody head off and said he hoped we gave them a good smack in the kisser.'

'He didn't!'

'He did. He never liked the Shaunnasseys. That is, he never liked their dad – "Old Nosy" he called him.'

'You've got a smashing dad.'

'He's not bad. What will your dad say?'

'Nothing. He's too busy reading Karl Marx. Me ma calls it trash. Me dad says it's the freedom of the masses from Capitalism, whatever that means.'

'Hey, wanna steal some golf balls?'

'Yeah, let's go.'

* * *

A twenty-pound note in England during World War Two was quite heavy with purchasing power. A Yankee soldier could inflatedly purchase four genuine bottles of Red Label scotch with it, the Kipper family could dine sumptuously with it for a fortnight, Uncle Bart could entertain the entire inhabitants of the Bird in Hand establishment for a night or two of jollity if he were so inclined, Saint Joseph's Academy of Hard Knocks could provide catechisms for the entire lower grades, or Sullivan and I could slurp ice cream for a month.

Uncle Bart had ten. They were brand new. They crackled like logs in a furnace. How he acquired them was a great mystery, known only to Black Bart and his supplier, clothed in utter secrecy, ten brand-new white twenty-pound notes. Should he have become the owner of this handsome legacy by legitimate means, that is, dint of hard labour, shoulder to the wheel, the knowledge would be common that Bart had been rewarded three months in arrears and three months in advance by a benign employer and he could thus venture handsomely into the world of commerce with his fortune.

But he did not spend one halfpenny. If he had a purse, it was tight shut. The ten bills crackled beneath his mattress. That is until one grey, foggy evening when he placed a bet on a mangy whippet named Dynamite down in the dell. It was owned by Cormac O'Flaherty, who bore a strange resemblance to his dog. 'I can't lose,' he whispered to Bart in his good ear. 'That's why I call him Doinomoit. He'll double your money.'

Now Bart Finnegan was as sharp as an Irish politician. But when it came to gambling, he was as dull as Maginnity's dog, which has never barked.

Placing a large percentage of his capital with bookie Seamus Kelly, he witnessed the whippet Dynamite take the lead, stop to scratch halfway, and then rejoin the race as the bobbies arrived, led by the red-nosed Inspector Callahan, who personally arrested Seamus Kelly, replete with all his money.

Bart disappeared over the railway track with several other pilgrims, arriving just at opening time of the Bird in Hand. 'Damn it!' said Bart. 'The drinks are on me, lads!' And that just about polished off his accumulated reserve.

'A foin man, that,' said O'Flaherty.

My father thought forgers were to be greatly admired, as much for their craft as their presumption. He said he always thought of them as smiling over their nocturnal labours, squinting through their multi-lenses at their product, nodding to one another at their fine craft, hoodwinking the Mother of Threadneedle Street into unfair exchange. 'It is one fine way,' he said, 'of thrashing the Capitalist system!'

'Isn't it stealing?' asked my mother, pouring hot water into the Waterford teapot.

This provoked my father into a gale of laughter. 'Stealing, woman? No, it's taking it back!'

From the cavern of his mature leather armchair he thrashed the *Liverpool Echo* about, reading again with great glee of the great forgery committed under the very noses of the city's constabulary. Oh, yes, they had discovered all the by-products, the incidentals; some of the paper, ink, and equipment; no plates; empty boxes; and no fingerprints. The counterfeiters had slipped away into the bleak night of yellow Liverpool fog many half-moons ago, for the forgeries were first-class, classic imitations, works of art, crackling twenty-pound notes already in fluid circulation.

Thus and so it was that Uncle Bartholomew Finnegan took a ferry boat, the *Royal Iris*, to Liverpool City. He wore his best cap, raked at a slight angle over his right eyebrow, jaunty, with white silk scarf knotted, *de rigueur*, round his neck. He needed to replenish his capital. It was a Monday morning washing day. 'Mary,' said he to my mother, Mary Catherine Kipper, nee Finnegan, 'I'd like to take young Tom with me to Liverpool tomorrow.'

'Tomorrow's Tuesday.'

'Aye.'

'He has school.'

'It will do the boy good,' answered Bart, cracking his knuckles. 'See a bit of the world.'

'On a boat? Across the Mersey?'

'Aye, it will broaden the intellect.'

'What about school?'

'It will be a geography lesson.'

Ma looked at Bart. She knew Bart Finnegan had schemed up a matter of some industry, juxtaposing the elements, plot and counterplot, and he needed another character – me – in his play, his Shakespearean theatrical. It was no use asking him; an evasive response had as much value as a Tory promise.

I sat at the kitchen table eating a salted potato.

'Tom, do you want to go to Liverpool tomorrow with your Uncle Bart, as if I didn't know the answer.'

'Yeah, Ma.'

'Don't say yeah! Don't use Americanisms in this house.'

The *Royal Iris* shook its timbers loose from the landing stage, turned with the tide, and careered downstream. The Liver buildings grew visually larger while seagulls wheeled, white and grey, with black eyes and orange beaks, then hovered like the Holy Spirit, crying at ingratitude. The pilot turned into the tide, nudging starboard into the side; up the gangplank we trod, Bart looking shrewd and happy, into the city.

Paradise Street was known to seafarers many generations gone, each generation improving its lot but keeping the original. The boarding houses became gin palaces, graduating to pubs with grained wood interiors, etched mirrors, and the pungent smell of good ale. Each has character. It was to an alehouse of bare floorboards, with steps worn down into the interior where we passed a statue of Queen Victoria with the porcelain chips missing from Her Majesty, that we ventured.

The cloth-capped men at the bar with polished elbows turned in unison as we entered. Through the smoke-filled gloom, a shaft of sunlight streamed from Paradise Street, behind which two men sat at a table in cavernous arm-chairs, wineglasses reflecting illumination from the street above.

Bart took my hand as we walked over to them and gripped their hands in salutation, the three men smiling.

'Who's this?' asked the tall one, the younger. I couldn't recognise his accent.

'This is Tom Kipper,' said Bart, 'my nephew. Came with me for the geography.'

But they did not ask me to sit down. 'Across the street,' said one to Bart, who beckoned me to follow him back into Paradise Street, where he pointed to the other side. 'Over there, Tom,' said Bart, 'is a bakery with apple tarts, mince pies, and even ice cream. Would you like to go across there for a while, while I talk to these gentlemen on a business matter? I shan't be long. Here's half a crown; get whatever you want.'

I looked in utter amazement at the silver he handed me, the royal head of George smiling on his money.

I slipped across the street and went down the steps into the Black Swan like a salt of yesteryear when Drake was a lad.

The young woman behind the counter had long eyelashes and green-grey eyes with a wisp of auburn hair hanging over her forehead. I said I'd like a chocolate-chip cone, which I would devour with all haste, while no one was looking, at a small marble table by the window looking out on to Paradise Street.

I was fascinated by two gorgeous objects: the oblong-shaped pastry behind the glass enclosure thickly oozing with cream and lemon custard, the pastry iced to crisp perfection; the second was the girl. I walked to the counter.

'Why are you looking like that?' she asked.

'Because you're beautiful,' I said.

She stared at me, grinning slowly and delightedly.

'What about the Napoleon?' she enquired.

'Napoleon?'

'That's what we call the pastry, a Napoleon.'

'It looks smashing.'

'I'll get you one.'

'How much?'

'It's on me. What's your name?'

'Tom Kipper.'

'Where are you from?'

'Across the water.'

'Well, all right. Be careful with the Napoleon. They can get pretty squishy, Tom.'

'Thank you, miss.'

She handed the pastry to me enclosed in a cardboard container.

At the door I looked back and found her looking at me, hands on hips, smiling.

I said, 'I'll pray to Saint Joseph for you.'

I put the box carefully under my jacket and stepped into Paradise Street.

Tramcars were whizzing past like Comanche arrows in a John Wayne movie.

* * *

Angels, the last of the third hierarchy of nine choirs, mused, reflected, and stirred their spiritual selves around a circular desk, not unlike Arthur's round table. They were junior angels, the last rung; they were awaiting advancement, awaiting assignments, and were moved with jocularity, joy, and, it must be admitted, some mischief. Didn't HE have a sense of humour?

Lipitor had the chair.

'Bartagna of Upper Echelon,' he said, 'has assigned me to England.'

'Isn't there a war going on there right now?' queried Elphreda.

'Yes, World War Two. They don't call it that but will later on.'

'What are you venturing there for, pray?' asked Elphreda.

'A young chap by the name of Tom Kipper, teenage – thirteen, fourteen, that is – being guided down a miscalculated path, a confused journey.'

'Doesn't he have parents?'

'They don't know exactly what he's doing. He's got to the stage where he thinks certain considerations are "almost true".'

'Ah, the "Almost True" stage,' said Elphreda. 'But isn't this of minor consideration for one of the nine choirs, even if we're on the tail end?'

'Well, Plutardinos has a soft spot for him!'

'Ah, Plutardinos.'

They broke up after the meeting, comparing notes over tea. 'Lipitor became an angel by some sort of default,' whispered Elphreda to Baggly. 'He's quite likely to mess this one up.'

'What time's your flight?' asked Charlie.

She wasn't there. Not a shadow. Bart had said that I would find her about the entrance to Finder's Keepers, a pub, crumbling but dignified, like Bart, with decades of graceful people swimming in wit with scarcely the price of a pint or a glass of brown ale but a treasury of compassion and laughter. This didn't do me any good as I searched the assigned territory without whimper or sign of the gracious lady described by Uncle Bart. That is, until I turned the corner at Wenlock Drive. The woman, Charlotte, was in the company of a large police constable and a shabby man wearing an unlaundered raincoat knotted about him with a belt of another hue. He was pure Humphrey Bogart.

I moved briskly in the opposite compass, past the O'Reilly Chippy, up Dolly Green Road, down Newcastle Court, up Brooks Hill, and past Shadwell Hall, until I was approaching Saint Joseph's Academy of Hard Knocks on Eastwick, my very own piece of civilisation. Furtively casting a glance over my shoulder, which is about the only way I could do it, I caught in my peripheral vision a shabby man in a shabby raincoat.

Saint Joseph beckoned me into the vaults of the church through the side entrance, past the ancient font of holy water, the stone flags, and brass door handles polished by generations of spirit-filled widows praying for brave husbands who had preceded them to Paradise but lost all that money on the football pools.

The church was in hushed splendour, one ray of silver sunshine slicing a beam into the rear pews and a small red lamp burning in a beaten copper compass. I walked towards the middle aisle then through swinging doors into the vestibule where on Sundays parishioners milled back and forth at the beginning and end of Masses. There was the echo of heels behind me; wearing a scruffy raincoat he was, going up the aisle, halting, uncertain. I took the box from under my coat, looked at it for a full five seconds, stripped off the cover with my Irish nails, and said the fastest Hail Mary of my life.

There were twenties and some fifties stuffed together with a red rubber band, thick as one of Ma's corned beef sandwiches. I blessed myself with the holy water, slid the bills out of the box, and replaced them with the pastry I had carried with me from Paradise Street, the ancient boulevard of mariners and villains.

The footsteps with the raincoat were pattering over to the side near the confessional boxes. I slipped open the opposite door, eased out to the side entrance in silence, and passed Our Lady of Sorrows into the anaemic English sunlight, smiling.

'Got you,' said the hand on my shoulder.

'Get your bloody hands off me!' I said.

'Tut, tut. You can tell that to the inspector at the station.' The large policeman I'd seen with Charlotte and

Humphrey Bogart came, breathing heavily, through the iron gate. 'I've got him,' said Bogart.

Craven Arms police station was just around Bletchley Corner, two streets away, which is where they guided my skinny Irish body up the steps and into the inspector's office.

'Tom Kipper,' said the inspector, after consultation with Bogart and Bobby, 'you have a package, a box, that we would like to see.'

'Wait 'til my dad hears about this,' I said.

'The box?' said the inspector. The Adam's apple in his scrawny neck jigged up and down like a corkscrew.

'What box?'

'The one under your jacket.'

It was my moment of triumph. I once heard Uncle Bart say, 'Every man in his time has fifteen minutes of glory!' I took out the box from under my arm. It was squished somewhat from its frantic journey, a tattered conveyance. Their eyes gleamed. Three pairs of policemen's eyes were in sheer delight. It was the policeman, the fat bobby, who took it, opened it on the inspector's desk, and drew forth a leaky, battered, creamy Napoleon.

Three pairs of glassy eyes looked at me.

'I'd like to go home now,' I said.

'The King's Catch' never caught on. The name, that is. As a commercial venture, it was a big winner; however, the establishment at the pier head became O'Reilly's Chippy from day one. Young Perrington O'Reilly deep-fried his cod with the fervour and elan of Michelangelo in the Vatican after a flagon of Sicilian vino.

O'Reilly, of course, was driven by common ale from the pub Finder's Keepers, teetering cheek by jowl next door way before the Irish came.

Uncle Bart's wife's (Isabelle's) niece, Charlotte – dark of hair, with a tan in her complexion, eyelashes like the portcullis on Glamis Castle, and deep, dark brown eyes on fire with whatever possessed her – became a constant customer of O'Reilly's Chippy. We failed at the time to discover if the attraction was for his generous chips or the way he gently passed her the cod after shaking the vinegar – who can tell with us Irish? We do know there was fire under the fish and chips. She looked something like her mother, Isabelle, black Irish, with mystery in the look and origins lost in the darkness of Gaelic history and Guinness.

'She was a lucky woman to get me brother Bart,' said my mother. 'But I don't know how she puts up with him. Pass the salt.'

Chips O'Reilly was poised with a flashing spatula in hand. 'My darling Charlotte,' he said, 'a chippy is not just a location where you pick up fish and chips. It is a social amenity of the same dimension and spirit as a great hotel, a public house, or a debating chamber.'

'Full of Greek gods from the ferry, I suppose, ready to fill their boots with common ale next door.'

'Possibly, possibly. Wine flowed freely in Athens.'

'Hear, hear,' said Francie Muldoon, who had just disembarked from the one-thirty. 'Give me the regular, Mr Chips.'

Charlie Magee, who awaited his order of chips and mushy peas, said, 'I've always been partial to your emporium, Mr Chips, with the nice people and good cod. What do you think, Francie?'

Francie was forty, had been since the previous week, and was with and without guile as the occasion demanded; she gave Charlie, divorced, a speculative eye. 'What do you think about buying a girl a beer next door, Mr Magee?'

Said Magee to Chips O'Reilly, 'Postpone two orders, Mr Chips. We shall return in about an hour or as fate decrees.'

As the door swung shut, Chips said to Charlotte, the only love of his life, 'You see what I mean?'

'Perry O'Reilly,' she answered, 'it just might interest you to know that several men of your own age – but not disposition – are interested in me. Visiting you every day in this common chippy is not my idea of inspiration or romance. Do you love me or do you love this common chippy?'

'Ah,' breathed Perrington. 'It's an engagement ring you're hankering after.'

'Not necessarily so,' hissed Charlotte. 'I just want to know your intentions; otherwise, it could be Goodbye Mr Chips!'

'And so you should,' said the stranger at the counter.

He was wearing a white jacket bearing the initials AMDG and a gold waistcoat.

'Who are you?' asked Chips.

'I'd like fish and chips,' he said. 'My name is Lipitor.'

'You're new here.'

'Was last here in 1888. Just came in on the boat.'

The telephone rang on the wall at the end of the counter. 'It's for you, Charlotte,' said Chips. 'It's Bart Finnegan.'

Charlotte didn't move. The stranger with the gold waistcoat and blue eyes said, 'You better take it.'

What was it about this fellow Lipitor?

'Hello,' she said into the phone.

'Hello, Charlotte, this is Bart. Can you do something for me?'

'How did you know I was here?'

'Aren't you always?'

'What can I do for you, Bart?'

'Young Tom Kipper will be catching the ferry, most probably at two o'clock. He will look for you outside the chippy or Finder's Keepers to give you a small box.'

'A box?'

'A box. A package. Can you look after it for me 'til tomorrow?'

'Of course, Bart.'

'It's quite valuable.'

'I'll look after it. Don't worry.'

'Got to go. 'Bye, Charlotte.'

'Bart wants me to meet Tom Kipper off the two o'clock,' she told Chips. 'See you later, Mr Chippy.'

* * *

Zachary Flanagan sipped from his pint glass of Guinness at the polished oak bar of the Finder's Keepers pub as Perrington O'Reilly stepped through the brass doors for a quick sip of ale, it being a task of great thirst to deep-fry those bales of Irish chips.

'Ah, Perry, me boy,' said Flanagan. 'Have you left the cod to swim by itself, have you?'

'I have and I haven't,' said Perrington. 'You're talking up such a storm I was wondering if you would be offering me the time of the day.'

'Give the poor lad a pint,' said Zachary Flanagan to the temporary barman these past three years, Seamus Doyle. They sipped and mused within for those first holy sixty seconds of the first pint of the day, dreaming of the glory of the Ireland they had left and were not in a rush to go back to.

'That Humphrey Bogart feller is making eyes at Charlotte round the corner on Wenlock Drive,' said Zachary Flanagan.

'What on earth are you talking about, Flanagan?' asked O'Reilly, sipping fast.

'There's a copper, too,' said Zachary. 'Big feller. Looks like he's using somebody else's ration book.'

'Round the corner, you say. On Wenlock?' He drank half the pint before coming up for air. 'You're talking about Charlotte Fossington?'

'Aye. Your Charlotte.'

'With a copper?'

'Aye.'

'A bloody copper?'

'Aye.'

'And a man wearing a dirty raincoat? And you didn't question these eejits?'

'I did not.'

Perrington O'Reilly moved with the speed of Irish beer. But it was too late, for the protagonists had gone in the spirit of the moment to Craven Arms police station, where the clientele claim the tea is weak.

'Are you looking for a young woman with black hair and black eyes?' asked the ancient lady on the bus bench. She had the wisdom of bus stop ages in her eyes.

'Brown eyes.'

'The very same.'

'You've seen her, lady?'

'Gone to Craven Arms with a big copper and a man in a scruffy raincoat.'

'You are an angel.'

Chips O'Reilly strode, almost ran, into the precinct at Craven Arms. 'On what charges are you holding this woman?'

'Who are you, may I ask?'

'Perrington O'Reilly.'

'And what relation are you to Charlotte Fossington?'

'I am her fiancé, which has absolutely nothing to do with present circumstances. I am also her legal counsel. Now, on what charges is she being held?'

The inspector looked forlornly at the squished Napoleon on his desk. 'She may go,' he said.

If he had a cloak, Perrington O'Reilly would have wrapped his beloved's shoulders with it in grand gesture, but all he had was a beige scarf keeping out the Mersey chill. He threw this round her gorgeous neck, steering her through the bleak station door into a starlit night.

Every woman in history knows when to be the gentler sex, to allow her hero to be chargé d'affaires, a Lancelot, and to say, 'We'll have dinner at Freddy's, OK?'

Out on the peninsula they occupied a table at river's edge where in yonder distance the lights of Liverpool glinted, the moon bent an elbow over the River Mersey, and stars splashed a fabled night, and she said, 'Who said I was your fiancée?'

'It's about time, Charlotte Fossington, that you became Mrs Chips. You can work for me. The pay is lousy.'

'I do,' she said.

'That legal counsel,' said the inspector, 'who is he really?'

'Chips O'Reilly, sir. Owns the chippy down at the pier head.'

'Yes, I thought I could smell mushy peas.'

'Tell me again,' said my mother, 'how you came to be at the Craven Arms police station.'

'I've told you six times, Ma!'

'You exaggerate just like your father. Tell me again.'

There was a loud knock on the front door.

'It must be your Uncle Bart. Let him in.'

'Hello, Mary,' said Bart.

'Take off your hat,' said Ma. She never, ever told anyone to take off a hat unless there was a glimmer in her heart that the hatted person was engaged in some unbeknownst manner in a matter not brilliantly clear to the innocent, unbeguiled world.

'Thomas,' she said to Bart, 'is just illuminating my inferior mind with details about his arraignment at Craven Arms.' She dashed a hot iron over a striped, colourless shirt.

'Mary,' said me dad from his leather armchair cave, 'is there any tea?'

'Ah,' breathed my mother, 'the prophet has awoken.'

'A cup of tea would be nice, Mary,' said Bart.

My mother poured the tea.

'There's going to be a fog tonight,' said Bart.

'There's a fog,' said my mother, 'right now, in this room.'

'I was coming off the two o'clock boat,' I said as soon as we were all supplied with cups of steaming orange pekoe and black tea, 'when a man in a raincoat started following me.'

'Yes,' said my mother's blue eyes. 'What then?'

Uncle Bart was sitting uneasily on the ancient davenport, creaking its springs, for he did not know what I was about to divulge.

'An angel named Lipitor told me to go to the church.'

The whole world stopped. My mother's eyes popped.

Uncle Bart went into a trance, his teacup perched perilously on the edge of the saucer.

'He said it was a safe haven – that's the words he used.' Nobody spoke, so I said, 'Honest!'

In her whole life, my mother has only once ever been short of something to say. This was it. It was writ in history. Empires fell. Kings were dethroned. Speech entered into oblivion. Me ma shut up.

'Did he have an accent?' asked Bart, for his world was crumbling; being a man of much enterprise, he had to swim or die.

'Does it matter,' Ma said to Bart, 'if the man had an accent, if he was an angel?' After she realised the whole conversation was developing the consistency of Scotch mist, she said to me, 'What did he look like?'

'He was wearing a scruffy raincoat.'

'I don't mean the man who was following you. I mean the angel. What did you say his name was?'

'Lipitor. He had blue eyes, kind of brown hair, and a white jacket with initials.'

'What kind of initials?'

'I think it was AMDG. And he had a gold waistcoat.'

My mother pursed her Irish mouth, uttered a great Gaelic sigh, and said, '*Ad marjorem Deum Gloria?* You're making this all up, aren't you, Tom Kipper?'

'I'm not. Honest, Ma.'

'Ah, the boy's telling the truth, Mary,' said Bart.

'And how would you know that, Bartholomew Finnegan?'

We sipped our tea.

'Why,' she asked, 'were you taken to Craven Arms?'

'They wanted to see what was in the box.'

'The box. What box?'

'The box Uncle Bart gave me.'

'So, Uncle Bart gave you a box. Now we're getting to the heart of the matter. And what did they find?'

'A Napoleon.'

'A Napoleon?'

'It was pretty squishy.'

'Uncle Bart gave you a squishy Napoleon?'

'Not exactly.'

'Meaning?'

'Well, it's almost true.'

'Tom Kipper, if I ever hear you say "almost true" again, you will eat cabbage every day for a whole month. I promise you.' Ma's cabbage was Purgatory on earth. It was dark green, almost black, wet, soggy, the consistency of an old horse, fetid, and brackish, a torture device of the Middle Ages.

'He gave me,' I shuddered, 'a box to take to Charlotte Fossington outside Finder's Keepers pub at the pier head.'

Hands on hips, she looked at me, eyes glittering. 'Are you talking about that black Irish woman, that niece of your Uncle Bart, the one with the eyes flashing at all the men?'

'I think so, Ma.'

'And what,' she asked, 'was in the box?'

'Well, Ma,' I said, 'Uncle Bart gave me half a crown for ice cream in Liverpool on Paradise Street.'

'Paradise Street? Half a crown for ice cream from Uncle Bart?' She wasn't screaming, although it contained a similar urgency.

'So I put the Napoleon from the ice cream parlour into the box in the church.'

'You didn't give the box to Charlotte Fossington?'

'No. I gave it to the big, fat copper at Craven Arms. He had a fit. He and the inspector and Humphrey Bogart.'

Bart started to laugh. Even my mother was beginning to smile. 'But what was in the box Uncle Bart gave you?'

My eyes closed. Moments of truth always hit you smack in the kisser. When I opened them, Bart was looking at me. 'Lots of twenty-pound notes.'

'Twenty-pound notes?'

'And a few fifties, I think.'

'It was a large bet I placed on a horse,' said Bart.

'Then why,' said my mother, shaking me, 'did you not give them to the police?'

'Because,' I said, 'they were Uncle Bart's.' Which made sense. Or so I thought.

'Is there any more tea?' asked my dad. Everybody looked at him.

'There's only one more thing,' said my mother. 'What did you do with the money?'

'Yes,' said Bart, 'the money.'

'I put it,' I said, 'in the poor box.'

The whole world screeched to a halt.

Putting something into the poor box was tantamount to execution at the guillotine, whether it was the coin of the realm, a promissory note, a love letter, a picture of Lord Roberts on horseback, or the *Liverpool Echo*. Once enclosed within the iron grip of the poor box, it passed into another dimension.

'I'm sorry, Uncle Bart,' I said.

'Ah, no need for sorrow, Tom Kipper,' said Bart. 'The canon will distribute the dividend like the chancellor of the exchequer. He might even buy himself a pint.'

My mother was looking at me with renewed interest. 'Did Uncle Bart give you a geography lesson?' she asked. 'And why are you limping?'

The angel Lipitor was most solicitous in advising me to seek the sanctuary of the church, but he never advised what I was about to reveal.

I sat in the squeaky, lumpy couch. Slowly I took off my left shoe, peeled off my smelly sock, and took out four twenty-pound notes. 'They wouldn't fit in the poor box,' I said.

'Holy Mother!' said my holy mother.

'You most splendid boy!' said Bart.

Everybody danced.

The canon got a new bike.

Ma got new slippers.

Bart got an ovation at the Bird in Hand when he announced, 'The drinks are on me.'

Chips O'Reilly got himself a wife.

Lipitor got new wings. Spiritual, mind you.
The *Liverpool Echo* got skidoo.
The forgers got five years.
And Tom Kipper got a geography lesson.
'All on my money,' said Bart.

Chapter Fifteen

Flanagan's Choice

'You can only use the adult library when you're sixteen, and I think you're not quite fourteen. Am I correct, Tom Kipper?' A chestnut wave of hair partly obscured her blue eyes that were capped by long lashes, sweeping upward to transfix me and downward to secretly smile at me. She was twenty-two years old. Sullivan and I were in love with her, and she knew it. So she smiled at us between checking out library books, battered by use, tattered corners (the books, I mean) waiting for the war to end.

'Her name's Priscilla Doherty,' I told Sully.

'Aye,' said Sully. 'She's twenty-two. Me ma told me.'

The library, tottering on the corner of Peckit Street and Priory Lane, was assembled in 1899 by Albert Fossdike and son between copious draughts of pale ale and building materials of miraculous substance, for it was still standing. The entrance of polished red brick had impressed above the pseudo-Gothic entrance a granite stone reading '1899 Fossdike'. The stone gleamed and the building sagged, like the Tory Party at prayer. When the bomb dropped that night, the entrance was left standing but the books were buried deep by the library of bricks.

My dad smiled, for he kept the three Dickens novels outstanding. '*Great Expectations*,' he murmured from his couch.

'The library's gone,' said Sullivan the morning after the raid. For the most part, all Sully and I could think of was when we would see Priscilla Doherty again. We went down to Priory Lane to examine the rubble and look for pieces of German shrapnel, searching studiously for bits bearing German insignia or numerals, which were sometimes higher in value than a new cricket bat or a Tory promise.

'Clear off!' said the police sergeant, an invitation that we completely ignored. 'Didn't you two hear what I said?' He raised his voice two notches.

'Yes,' said Sully, 'and we're taking no notice!'

That was when we fled down a side alley by Peckit Street leading to Saint Joseph's Academy of Hard Knocks, where we were receiving (or not) our final year of education before terrorising the world.

'Did you notice,' asked Sully, 'the Yankee soldier on the corner over by the bank?'

'Aye, I did.'

'Let's go see if he has any chewing gum.'

So we trod back onto Priory Lane from the alley and

up to the corner where we saw the Yank leaning on the red pillar-box. 'Yeah,' he answered, giving us each a stick of peppermint from a top pocket. He seemed to be about the age of my brother, Matt Kipper, who was on a Navy ship in the Atlantic sinking a U-boat a day. The Yank seemed very friendly.

'Hey,' he said, as we chewed like mad. 'You guys know anything about Priscilla? She used to be in the library.'

'Yes,' we answered.

'Know where she lives?'

'No.' We shook our heads.

'Hmmm. Can you find out?' He patted his pocket.

'Have you got any cigarettes?' asked Sully.

He leaned on the pillar-box and laughed. 'Yeah, I got cigarettes.'

'I can ask me ma,' I said. 'She knows everything.'

'Listen,' he said, bending down to be closer to us. 'If you can find out anything about her, I'll make it worth your while.' He took out a pen and wrote a telephone number on the back of a Camel cigarette packet. 'I'm stationed at the PX in Liverpool. Give me a call there, and I'll really appreciate it.' He straightened up. 'What are your names?'

'I'm Tom Kipper and this is Sully.'

'My name is Joe Serrano, and I gotta go catch that ferry boat; I'm on duty.'

'I'll give you a call from a telephone box,' I said.

'Thanks, guys.' The look in his eyes was haunting. He walked quickly down Priory Lane.

'He's going to miss the boat,' said Sully.

'Hey,' I said, 'before we go home, let's give a razz to that bloody copper!'

Which we did.

While the village still slept in those wee hours of the morning, when leprechauns work a magic unknown to common man, a Yankee soldier in U.S.-issue boots padded up Priory Lane, with great stealth picked his way across mounds of shining red bricks, and commenced to excavate. He had worked perhaps one hour in tragic search for his vanished love when PC Moynihan breezed by, puffing up the hill. 'You can't go behind the fences, sir,' said the squat policeman, the one with the tight collar strangling him into retirement. 'What do you want, anyway?'

'I'm looking for the librarian, the woman, Miss Priscilla Doherty; she was here when the bomb fell.'

'You must be mistaken, sir. The building was empty.'

'She was working overtime.'

'No, sir, you're wrong. Now would you please get behind the fences; the sergeant will be very annoyed if he sees you here.'

'I'll just look through these bricks.'

PFC Joe Serrano of the PX in Liverpool couldn't be controlled, cajoled, seduced, or wheedled into extracting his U.S. Army boots from the mountain of red bricks at Priory Lane Corner until Sergeant Rodney Moriarty induced him by physical reasoning. He ended up – both of them, that is – at Craven Arms police station.

'I love her,' said PFC Joe Serrano.

'Would you like another cuppa tea?' asked the sergeant.

As Serrano's most secret agent, I was grilling my mother.

'She lives by herself on Saint Mary's Lane,' Ma said. 'Why do you want to know?'

'An American soldier was asking.'

'What did he look like?'

'Like an American soldier.'

'Don't you get smart with me, Tom Kipper, or I'll box your ears!'

'Well, he looked kind of worried, Ma. Said his name was Joe Serrano, and he would give us some gum and cigarettes if we found Miss Doherty.'

'And he's going to give cigarettes to children?'

'To Sully, Ma. I didn't ask him.'

'Oh, no, you're an angel. I'll speak to Mrs Sullivan about this.'

'Can I tell him?'

'Tell who what?'

'Can I tell the Yank where she lives?'

'I suppose so. Let me know what he says.'

I telephoned Joe Serrano from a telephone box at Shepherd's Corner, and then I met him at the pier head. This was after he and Sergeant Moriarty enjoyed orange pekoe tea together down at the Craven Arms police station.

When I met him at the pier head not far from

O'Reilly's chippy, he looked as if he hadn't been sleeping much. On an inside page of the *Liverpool Echo*, he showed me an article headlined 'Local Woman Librarian Goes Missing After Raid'.

'She's under those bricks,' he breathed heavily. 'I know she is.'

'She lives on Saint Mary's Lane,' I said.

'Saint Mary's Lane?'

'Yes, my mam told me.'

'Is it far away?'

'No. Just past the village.'

At number four Saint Mary's Lane, several older people were gathered, all talking at once in the front garden. No one was taking any notice of the others, like politicians' wives, or so it seemed to me; that is, until they saw Joe Serrano in his uniform and they all stopped to look at him.

A greying man with uncontrolled fuzzy eyebrows detached himself from the group to advance menacingly on Joe Serrano. 'Are you,' he said, 'the American soldier who's been seeing my daughter, Priscilla?'

'I didn't know she was your daughter, sir.'

'Well, she is. Have you any idea where she is?'

'You don't know?'

'Would I be asking you if I knew?' His eyebrows flew in various compass directions.

'Why don't you ask the poor wee man in for a cuppa tea?' said the angelic lady at his elbow. 'And the wee boy, too.'

Joe removed his cap as he entered the front parlour and saw her picture, a glossy film, on the mantel shelf. 'Joe Serrano,' she had said to him, 'you are in such a hurry; I do not think you are a nice person to know.' Tears, the riptide of a woman's emotion, flooded those startlingly blue eyes. 'You are most probably married. Maybe twice. You think I will get myself emotionally entangled with an American soldier from Los Angeles I hardly know? I let you kiss me – just once, mind you – and you make the most unseemly proposition to me. I am completely at a loss for words!' The tears came storming in like high tide on the Mersey.

'All I asked,' said Joe Serrano, 'is will you marry me?'

But she was gone, gone in a great flurry of legs, hips, and sniffles, out through the door of the cafe, and nobody ever saw her again.

'I think she's trapped under those bricks at the library,' he said to her father, Frank Patrick Doherty; her mother, Margarita; her brother, Seamus; her sister Lottie McCabe; and her next-door neighbour, Jimmy Malone.

'You know,' said Seamus, 'he might, just might, have a point. You can't trust those Sherlocks and Watsons at Craven Arms station. They can't find her. Let's look into the library.'

It was a motley crew that advanced, sleeves rolled up, on the bombsite at Peckit and Priory, with no tools, but strong Irish backs, grasping fingers, and perspiration. They toiled, heaved, and flung bricks with seemingly reckless intent, shouting encouragement. Sergeant Rodney

Moriarty arrived in half an hour, telephoned by O'Brien ('Fish') down the street who said that a school of foreign archaeologists were excavating the ruin.

'Hey, listen here,' shouted the sergeant, dropping his bicycle, 'you're trespassing on private property.'

'She's buried in the rubble,' said Frank Patrick Doherty.

'Who is?'

'My daughter, Priscilla.'

'How do you know that?'

'Ask Seamus, me son, over there. Would you get off those bricks.'

Taking his helmet off, Sergeant Rodney Moriarty scratched a shock of red hair.

'Here's her lunch bag!' screamed Margarita Doherty.

The cadre of diggers, Sergeant Moriarty included, scrambled over heaps of red bricks to survey the evidence.

'Let's concentrate here,' shouted Joe Serrano.

'And you've got a bloody Yank with you, too,' said the sergeant, rolling up his sleeves.

Father Nicholas O'Toole, five months out of Ballyporeen Seminary, thrown headlong into England by his sniffy superiors, stumbled into the brick mountain on sturdy Irish legs. 'What the divil,' sez he (I am positively assured that it is what he said), 'is going on here?'

'A woman,' said Jimmy Malone, 'a libarian, is buried beneath the mound.' The young priest, muscled from hurley, jumped leprechaun-like into the bricks.

Uncle Bart Finnegan, going nowhere in particular but

wearing an aura of executive restraint, almost fell into the library. Apprised of the human tragedy, he rolled his shirt-sleeves up his beige arms to throw bricks with great exactitude – not too fast but neatly.

O'Brien, Fish, next to Boots the chemist, advised by the cobbler, O'Flaherty, closed down his aromatic parlour with a great clang to join the Priory diggers.

Fog, spectre-like, rolled down the Mersey, enveloping immense merchant vessels and the bleak wharves, wreathing the Liver Building and the half-built gothic cathedral, sneaking, rolling stealthily over the village and up Priory Lane at its own humorous pace, smiling. The pale sunlight that remained melted into the Irish Sea, which was when the last brick had been flung. Standing, Bart Finnegan said, 'Flanagan's Choice is just round the corner.'

It was a fine group of warriors that trooped into the adjacent tavern. With great English aplomb and Irish thirst, PFC Joe Serrano dug deeply into his allotment from the U.S. Mint.

Blanche Mulrooney pulled the pumps with muscles bigger than a docker's lunch as the Priory diggers sat in great splendid silence, defeated but unbowed.

'You'd better go home,' said Uncle Bart on the steps of the pub. I was four years short of admittance.

The number four bus pulled onto the pavement out of the fog with passengers spilling out – women in coloured headscarves, men in great raincoats – tumbling into the mist. Foghorns ghosted up the river. She stepped down carrying a small leather suitcase, moving with the gracious style of a ballerina on the Saturday afternoon matinee at the Roxy. She wore a Robin Hood hat and a black-and-white chequered coat pulled tightly round her waist. She was beautiful. But her attention became riveted on the valleys and hills of gleaming red bricks that had, two nights past, been the library. 'What happened?' she muttered hoarsely as she grabbed my arm with her beautiful fingers.

'A bomb dropped in the air raid,' I answered.

'Great merciful heavens!'

I was supporting her. I picked up her bag, which was now on the pavement. 'Would you come with me, miss?' I asked.

She followed me up the steps of Flanagan's Choice, through the lounge, still holding my arm, and into the bar. All eyes of the Priory diggers turned to me and my companion. Amateur theatricals coursed through my Irish blood. It was my finest entrance.

'Look, folks,' I said.

'Priscilla!' screamed her mother.

The whole building shook with cries of delight, rivers of tears, and the banging of beer glasses on tables as the ghost of Priscilla Doherty walked into the room. And when the cries had subsided a notch, it was the Yankee, Joe Serrano, who took her in his arms – and it was where she fled – knowing that her answer was now yes, Joe Serrano, I will marry you. 'I went to see Uncle Llewellyn in Llangollen,' she told her mother and father. 'I needed some advice.'

'Why didn't you come to me, my darling?' asked her father, Frank Patrick Doherty.

'And why, in heaven's great name, would anyone go to you for advice, Mr Doherty?' fretted her mother, Margarita.

'The drinks are on me again,' shouted Joe Serrano.

'A foin man, that,' said Uncle Bart Finnegan.

They let me stay in the bar, even Sergeant Rodney Moriarty, for I was, in a way, a kind of minor hero.

Mr and Mrs Joe Serrano thought so, anyway.

And that was how, at the age of fourteen, I lost my first love, married at Saint Joseph's Church, right next door to the Academy of Hard Knocks. In later years, Flanagan's Choice still tottered in Priory Lane. There is a picture hanging on the west wall of the bar, showing a Yankee soldier and his bride, an angel in shining white.

Underneath the picture is an inscription, brass letters on mahogany, reading, 'Into This Room Walked the Ghost of Priscilla Doherty.'

Drink a pint or two there, and you'll never feel the same again.

Even in Mersey fog.

Chapter Sixteen

The Big Cabbage

♣

We were the Academy Warriors. Thirteen years of age, crowding fourteen, confined to Saint Joseph's Academy of Hard Knocks, growing like weeds, full of blarney, tougher than the Wehrmacht hovering down there on the Channel coast of France like vipers, wearing long boots and short memories. If they met us, they'd be deader than Monday's *Liverpool Echo*, a daily piece of literature that smelled like old railway and turned brown in one day, like Uncle Bart's good intentions.

The year 1940 was kind of a mediocre, excitingly weird year. Evangeline O'Malley, 'neat as a new pin', said, 'He lost his parents, his whole family, and his entire memory, so we have to help him.'

'Help who?' asked Sully, spitting accurately into the gutter.

'Good shot, Sul,' I said.

'Oh, you horrid boys!' said Evangeline O'Malley.

'Who are you talking about, Vange?' I asked.

'Don't call me Vange. It's Evangeline to you two.'

'OK, Vange.'

'Do you want me to tell you or not?'

'OK, Vange – I mean Evangeline.'

'They could have been killed defending our own country,' she said, 'or Percival could have just lost his memory.'

'Percival?'

'Yes, he's in Beaney Meaney's class.'

'You mean Dotty Lotty.'

Evangeline O'Malley turned her spotted Irish nose up at this (a nose that in later years would drive me crazy). 'Well, you boys, he's all alone in this world, so treat him kindly!'

'Sounds like *Oliver Twist*,' I said to Sully.

Percival Partridge was an unusual kid, and Saint Joseph's Academy of Hard Knocks bred, nurtured and then spat out unusual kids. But this boy didn't even speak like us. He had no Merseyside accent. In those halcyon days, we didn't know we had 'Mersey' accents. We just knew Perce was almost a foreigner.

'Perhaps he's a Nazi agent,' said Sully.

But 'Perce' bled into the community, was a whiz at cricket, scored goals, and fascinated Vange O'Malley, who imitated his accent, closing her eyes a fraction and tilting her nose.

Something bothered us, something hard to put your

finger on, like a scratch you can't reach or a rule you couldn't break but weren't told why, or a big jelly in the cupboard that nobody ever ate, or being unable to hit your sister because she was a girl. But when I think of it, Sully and I would have gone to war for Vange O'Malley, even though she imperiously pronounced moral rectitude on all our activities. She was like a guardian angel in a gym slip.

Perhaps it was hypnosis with Percy Partridge. When he spoke, we listened, mouths open, Mersey glaze over the eyeballs. Then he would walk away and we could fight over the ball and the wicket again. He was almost a jailer.

After he had been discovered wandering along the beach without shoes, hair distressed, blown by the elements, he was picked up by our brave constabulary. Exactly the same would have happened to Sully and me should the same conditions have existed, but the bobbies would have stuck us in detention and advised quite mad parents that they had daft kids.

But they gave Percy Partridge orange pekoe and black tea, apple pie, a new cardigan, tennis shoes, cotton socks, and a home in a kind Catholic shelter run by the nuns.

Miss Meaney had him read to all the class. His diction was perfect, tonal quality first class. 'Sounds like that fart on BBC News,' said Sully. Beaney Meaney gushed over him like custard drowning a pie. He sat on the front bench with all the girls.

'I think,' said Sully, 'I'm gonna be sick.'

Vange O'Malley became a disciple of Percy Partridge, which drove us to utter distraction. I had remained on neutral ground, more or less, until one fateful day in the back schoolyard behind the library when Vange mentioned without guile that my surname was Kipper. Percy enunciated, 'Tom Kippah, Kip-pah,' like Winston Churchill or Henry the Eighth, so that my blood, wild ninety-nine per cent Irish, rose to a boiling point. I was going to stab him in a major artery with my sharpened carpenter's pencil. I was clutching pencil in fist when Sully held me back because he did not assassinate in such Irish fashion but planned death to dictators with great stealth and guile, bit by horrible bit, 'til they begged for mercy, which he did not give. I was a complete amateur by comparison. He would have made a great hit man for Henry the Eighth.

'We'll kill the bastard later,' said Sully.

That very evening at a local hostelry, wreathed in embracing fog, Uncle Bart was also engaged in drama, that of cabbage.

Seamus Haggerty had the biggest cabbage in the county. It was round, firm, and huge, almost more than Haggerty could heft, but he did, and he brought it into the inner sanctum of the Bird in Hand, where he hoisted it onto the bar. Brendan Mulrooney was not pleased. The bar was for serving pints of ale and stout to the thirsty men of the town and county, and as far as the chief barman was concerned, the cruciferous, smelly, spongy cabbage took up valuable space. 'Would you get it off the bar, Seamus,' he pleaded.

Seamus Haggerty had brought the cabbage up from the Dirty Duck where it had enjoyed great prestige on the only bar. Toasts had been offered to its girth and weight, and pints had been pushed copiously into the hands of Seamus so that he swam gilded in a sea of pride, dignity, hubris, joy, and beer. He therefore did a most admirable ballet step when he conveyed his cabbage from inn to inn. 'I've brought me cabbage,' said he, 'me magnificent, kelly-green cabbage, to show you all what will win most handsomely the Dig for Victory competition at the county fair tomorrow.' He leaned on his cabbage for support.

'It's hollow,' said Uncle Bart.

All eyes, reflecting green from the cabbage, turned to Bartholomew Finnegan.

'And what would you know about it, Bart Finnegan?'

Seamus towered above Bart, by comparison a small figure in homespun tweed, Donegal cap at rakish angle, elfish face, with charm and style befitting a man who knew the man who had the second largest cabbage in the county.

'This cabbage,' said Bart, 'is hollow. I have tested it.' He swallowed a draught from his porter.

Seamus Haggerty laughed, not too loudly, for it was an uncertain laugh. Bart Finnegan somehow seemed to be an authority on so much Bird in Hand history, drama and fable. 'And what, may I ask, did you test it with, Mr Finnegan?'

All cabbage green eyes switched back to Bart. There was a silence – no coughing and no unseemly laughter. Here was history unfolding. 'I tapped it,' said Bart, 'with me index finger, just once, mind you, with me ear glued to its leaf. And I ask anyone here in this pub to do the same, and he will hear a dull, hollow echo.'

'You're crackers,' said Haggerty. 'Give me another bottle of that stout.'

But the audience stood, rooted to the beer-stained boards.

'I'll try it out,' said Michael Laverty, 'presuming you don't mind, Seamus.'

'What a lot of blarney,' ground out Seamus Haggerty. 'How can this splendid cabbage I've grown me very self be hollow? And what in tarnation difference does it make anyway?'

'A fine point,' said Bart. 'I might remind you that in the Dig for Victory competition, it is mandatory that all cabbages be weighed, measured, and lastly sliced to ensure there is an inside. That it's not hollow. It's a regulation.' He sipped porter.

'All right,' said Seamus. 'Michael Laverty can tap the cabbage and listen. Saints be praised, he listens to a lot of other people's business anyway.'

The audience murmured approval. 'Would you shut off the radio?' said Laverty.

Silence crept into the bar. The door squeaked open and somebody told somebody to shut up.

Laverty cleared his throat, shrugged his shoulders, bent

his ginger head over the damp bar, pressed his left ear to the cabbage, settled himself gently, raised his right hand, and tapped the cabbage with his forefinger. Once he did and waited. You could hear the noise of traffic on Belvedere Boulevard but not a tinkle in the inner sanctum of the Bird. They waited.

Laverty extended his hand and tapped again. Then he straightened up, adjusted his cap and scarf, and cleared his throat. He said, 'It's hollow!'

The ensuing noise brought customers pushing in from the lounge bar. 'What's happening?' they asked.

'Seamus Haggerty's cabbage is hollow,' was the cry.

Seamus Haggerty, cabbage grower extraordinaire, did a brand-new ballet step, rolled his bloodshot Donegal eyes, and banged his fist upon the bar, spilling froth from pints of good ale, to bellow, 'I'll show you – I'll prove to you it's not hollow, you eejits!' He strode over to retired plumber Harry Kinneally and plunged a hand into the greasy bag of tools he carried forever with him, emerging with a short crosscut saw.

The cabbage gave to the slashing saw. It bled green. A mellifluous aroma spread to all the Irish noses, and the two sides fell, rocking sideways on the mahogany bar. The cabbage's interior was ringed light green and dark and pale, a pure delight of radiant colour. And it was not hollow. 'There you are, Bart Finnegan!' hoarsely screamed Seamus Haggerty.

But Bart was gone, already treading the cobbles of Belvedere Boulevard, wreathed in Mersey fog. And smiles.

* * *

Many counties south in this royal realm of kings, the fourth earl of Tewkesbury seethed also in drama. Sir Geoffrey Langtry said, 'I think we've found your son.'

'Oh, where is he? Where is the dear boy?' shrilled Charlotte, countess of Blackthorpe Manor.

'Somewhere in Liverpool in a home for Catholic orphans. You should never have introduced him to amateur theatricals, Charlotte. The boy's only half with us.'

'Thank God. Is he safe?'

'Safe? He thinks he's Oliver Twist.'

'Oh, my poor child. When will we see him?'

'I'm going up there tomorrow to judge a Dig for Victory competition, the largest cabbage category. Will pick the brat up then.'

'He's your son, too, Geoffrey.'

'Sometimes I wonder,' said Sir Geoffrey Langtry, fourth earl of Tewkesbury. 'That boy is much like your Aunt Matilda. Quite potty.'

Several green and ancient English counties north, Percival Partridge, fifth earl of Tewkesbury, was wallowing in the dubious ecstasy of Beaney Meaney's gushing dispensations. Miss Meaney's eyes glowed like those of a large dead halibut, for she was about to enlarge on a matter dear to her cantankerous heart: her favourite pupil. It was not, of course, the same pupil, for as the terms passed and her heart grew fonder, they progressed into the great beyond with her magical blessings while the remaining ninety-nine per cent fired rubber bands and spilled ink, thus receiving in return the displeasure of her carpenter's pencil upon their bony Irish knuckles.

'Children,' said she, 'as you know, I gave you an essay to write upon what you intended to be your career, your profession, your calling in life when you eventually leave Saint Joseph's. Well,' she further gushed, 'one of our pupils has created a most excellent essay. One of you boys has excelled. I am now going to call upon him to read his essay, so put down your pencils, put your hands together upon your desk, and listen most attentively to Percival Partridge read his masterpiece.'

'Do you mean Allover Twist, miss?' asked Sully.

'Report to me after class, Francis Sullivan. Now, Percival, read your essay.'

All the girls in the class looked at Allover Twist, as we called him. But we knew – and Beaney Meaney knew – that was not his real name; we knew that he came from Essex or Sussex or one of those funny places down there in the south of England where they slew dragons and rescued maids in distress. It was in the history books and our Saturday comics. And they were coming to get him. He thought he was Oliver Twist. Our minds boggled.

'My essay,' enunciated Percival Partridge, 'is entitled "When I Leave School I'm Going to Become a Priest".'

'He's bloody daft,' breathed Sully.

The essay delighted Beaney Meaney; it rolled like a great tide of sticky treacle, obliterating us common kids of common destiny, reaching halfway where Percy Partridge becomes a cardinal, and through it all Beaney Meaney simpered.

'She's as daft as he is,' further commented Sully.

'And that is why,' enunciated the great imperious Cardinal Partridge, 'that when I become a priest I will never be able to marry one of you girls.'

I saw Vange O'Malley in my peripheral vision, for the cardinal was looking at her, and I could not for the life of me understand the expression on her face. O'Malleys are like that.

'What will you charge for confession?' asked Sully.

'Stand in the back of the classroom,' shrilled Beaney Meaney.

The doorbell rang and a man entered dressed in a beige-coloured uniform up to his collared neck; a peaked cap, which he removed; and black, shiny black, gaitered boots. 'Excuse me, Miss Meaney; transportation is here for Master Clayton.'

'We shall be along shortly,' simpered Meaney.

The man smiled at us all and left.

'Children,' she said, 'Percival is leaving for home in the south of England, for he is here on a very short duration. A car is waiting for him at the side entrance. Let us all go down to see him off to his home.'

Master Clayton, son of the fourth earl of Tewkesbury, had been on his way home after his amateur dramatist, Oswald Swansdown, told him he was a great actor. This was after an afternoon of four, maybe five gin and tonics at the Nag's Head in Tooting on Lyme and a hefty largesse from Lady Charlotte, countess of Tewkesbury, after three Scotch on the rocks and two Guinness. Oswald was the perfect chauffeur. Clayton Langtry had therefore decided to become Oliver Twist for the sake of his theatrical blood.

'Sir Geoffrey,' said the chauffeur to Miss Meaney, 'is judging a cabbage contest at the Dig for Victory exhibition in the county park, so I shall deliver Master Clayton to him.'

We all followed them both down the hall passageway; through the cloakroom; out into the back schoolyard; past the comfortable, solid sandstone nave of the church; and to the gate leading into Shelbourne Alley. There, a large black chrome and brass Rolls-Royce was parked like a mighty ship, like the *Queen Mary*. We gawped. Percival Partridge strode forward to the gate as we all stopped. Turning, he announced in loud tones that it had been a pleasure meeting us all and that we were jolly good chaps.

'Shall I kill the bastard now?' seethed Sullivan.

Fate, the ultimate agency, divine will, perhaps providence stepped in, for Master Clayton, aka Allover Twist, bent to adjust his boot lace before he entered that ship of state, the Rolls-Royce, and his gluteus maximus, known to Merseyside peasantry as the large arse, a celestial sphere that required climactic termination, loomed into prominent perspective. It was not I. It was not Sullivan. With the greatest of deadly accuracy, she tippied up on her shiny, black, immaculate gym shoes and delivered a kick of sweet dimension smack on the target. A lot of muscle and disgust went into that kick and a lot of laughs. The future earl of Tewkesbury did a most splendid nosedive smack into the wing where he lay bawling, aristocratic blood oozing through his schnozz. Vange got it bad from Beaney Meaney and the headmaster, for it was usually ragged urchins like Tom Kipper and Sullivan who were disciplined while girls were always looked upon as ladies. Vange took our hearts after that, and we even dared to put our arms round her shoulders. And, you know what? She let us.

Five minutes after I got home, my mother, Mary Catherine Kipper, nee Finnegan, said, 'Well, did nothing happen today?'

This was an open invitation to provide some extraneous material for her next tea and buttered scones bash with Aunts Moira and Madge and the little lady from the corner, Buffin McCoy.

So I elaborated on the damage to the fifth earl of Tewkesbury's posterior, illustrating the rugby kick with overabundant elan.

'A blow for the working classes,' said my recumbent dad from his cave-like armchair.

'And the boy's father wasn't there?' asked my mother.

'No. The chauffeur said he was at the county fair judging cabbages. Can I go over there with Sully, Ma?'

'You may, just so long as you're back before dark or your father falls out of his armchair.'

We found Uncle Bart with Michael Laverty at the

bandstand beside which a portable bar had been erected (without outdoor licence), well taken advantage of by members of the brass band who appeared eminently disposed to spilling beer in their instruments, for musicians live in a world awash with oddities. The oboe player was asleep but still clutching with his left hand his instrument and right his beer bottle, snoring. Bart sat on a nearby park bench sipping Guinness.

It was summer splendour creeping into the County Park that day, a caressing, soft breeze under the giant oaks whispering memories of summers long past, a mellifluous mixture, sad and glorious.

Bird in Hand patrons sat on aged wooden benches, sipping bottled ale, surrounding Bart Finnegan and Michael Laverty. 'They're breaking the law,' said PC Malone. 'Shall I write them up, Sarge?' He unbuttoned the flap of a top pocket.

'Well, now,' puffed Sergeant Eugene O'Kelly. 'We should and we shouldn't.'

'How's that, Sarge?'

'Well, most of those men, including that woman, Polly Muldoon, are patrons of the Bird. Let me whisper to you, PC Malone: in undercover work for the force, it is sometimes most necessary to mingle with the lower strata of society to gain information leading to apprehension of unsavoury elements in the civilised world. Do I make myself clear, Mr Malone?'

'Aye, Sergeant. Yes, you do.'

'Then I suggest, Mr Malone, you go across to the

bandstand and speak with that little man in the centre of the group. His name is Finnegan. Tell him you're appropriating two bottles of ale for quality testing. Mention my name. He'll understand. Wrap the evidence, best you can, in that large handkerchief of yours and bring them to the woodshed at the rear of the art school. Understand me, Mr Malone?'

'Oh, yes, Sergeant!'

'A bird fancier I know,' said Bart, 'bought an exotic parrot at a pet shop in Liverpool.' He was talking to Michael Laverty. Everybody listened. We moved closer. 'It never stopped talking and singing, so he bought it for two hundred pounds and took it home to his wife, Glynnis. But for a whole month it never uttered a chirp, never said a word, so he took the parrot back to the shop, demanding a refund. "We never give refunds," said the owner. "Company policy. But I'll tell you what I'll do for you: I'll give you one hundred pounds and take it off your hands." Grumbling, as soon as the man took the hundred pounds and left the store, the parrot squawked, "That'll be fifty to me and fifty to you!"'

Bird in Hand patrons roared the applause of laughter and Bart smiled, slurping Guinness.

The earl of Tewkesbury raised his hand at the podium situated in an acre of God's green earth at the county fairground. Cabbages littered oblong-shaped trestles for many hundreds of yards, and gardeners of all dimensions waited for the verdict. 'The winner,' said Sir Geoffrey

Langtry, 'is a man who has gardened all his life, he tells me. Well, he must have done, for he has produced the most magnificent cabbage I have seen for many years.' A great cheer rang out. 'I have the great privilege of awarding this certificate and this monetary prize to the man who has grown the largest cabbage in this county, none other than Michael Laverty.' The earl placed the seal on the lapel of Laverty's jacket, handing him his reward – a check for one hundred pounds.

Moving closer, Uncle Bart whispered in the ear of Laverty at the bar, 'That'll be fifty to you, Michael, and fifty to me.'

And so a great quiet descended upon Saint Joseph's Academy of Hard Knocks, for the Hun was at the door looking for a foothold, aeroplanes occasionally rent the skies, and we were on the last leg of our term before we quit to take on the 'career' that Beaney Meaney was forever on about.

The package that came in the post office van, delivered to the headmaster's office, was actually addressed to Evangeline O'Malley and was sent by the fourth earl of Tewkesbury. 'Pop' Devereaux gave it to Vange without asking her to open it, for he would find out sooner or later from his gossip patrol.

Sully and I hemmed her in at the wall in the playground next to the church. 'What's in it, Vange?' we asked.

'Wouldn't you like to know?'

'That's why we're asking.'

'Well, I don't know.'

'Why don't you open it?'

'Because it's private.'

But she did open it because Vange knew we were her knights in rusty armour. It was a monster box of assorted chocolates, which only earls and dukes could get in wartime Britain. With it was a note, which she read aloud: 'Dear Miss O'Malley, You have most probably been disciplined by your superiors for the swift kick in the pants you gave to my son. Well, I want you to know I was delighted. I still am. Taught him a fine lesson. Tell your folks if they are ever down here in Sussex to look us up and drop in for tea. Best regards, Sir Geoffrey Langtry, Earl of Tewkesbury.'

We had one chocolate each and then Vange started crying. After she left through the big gates to go home, I asked Sully, 'What was she crying for?'

'Who knows?' said Sully. 'Who can understand girls?'

It was many years later in the corner of some forgotten field that will be forever England when I received a scissored slice of *Liverpool Echo* obituaries advising the passing on to Glory of Seamus Haggerty.

Patrons of the Bird in Hand thought he was leaning two elbows on the bar with his pint glass of porter – emptied of course – by his side, but he had moved into greener cabbage patches. A fine Requiem Mass was celebrated at Our Lady and Saint Joseph Church, nudging elbows with the Academy of Hard Knocks, Uncle Bart a pallbearer hefting the box, thence to interment at Hake Lane Cemetery.

Inscribed on his tall tombstone are the words:

> A Haggerty man, name of Seamus
> Here he lies somewhat in sorrow
> Not unknown – but not quite famous
> He never discovered if a cabbage was hollow.

The Bird stayed open an extra hour to refresh mourners.

Chapter Seventeen

Pilgarlic?

'She looks like a Pilgarlic!'

'Ma, what's a Pilgarlic?'

She scrubbed the inside of the pot which already had a sheen as bright as sparkling silver.

Ma gave me that special Irish look she had; it meant that she was sizing me up; was he the wee boy of yesteryear or had his brain exploded to Scouse proportions at the Academy of Hard Knocks? For nobody had ever asked her that question. It hung in the air like a rusty guillotine or dirty drawers. Just to ask the question meant you were minus normal nervous tissue in the skull. Didn't it? Perhaps you were a Pilgarlic. This was the reason nobody had ever asked the question. And Ma, being Ma, had to answer.

'Why don't you go out to play cricket with Patrick Kinneally!'

Late that very afternoon, ladies of related tribal influence met in Mary Catherine Kipper's living room for gallons of tea and crumpets. Only after the first sip of satisfying Pekoe and Black did they gather their sublime intellect to discuss most important matters, the leading two being, one, how to deal with husbands of impaired intellect and grubby table manners, and two, what is a Pilgarlic. Miraculously a bottle of sherry appeared. All her life Mary Kipper had employed Pilgarlic to many and sundry matters, dispensations and to her offspring. Nobody ever disputed her largesse with Pilgarlic. But where were its origins, from what, perhaps foreign, field did it emanate; perhaps Latin or Greek or Hindustani or even Gaelic.

'Me dad,' said Auntie Madge, 'used the expression in the pub at home in Tipperary.'

'It's Irish, then,' announced Zelda Sweeney, sipping her tea from her china cup.

'I knew a horse in Antrim named Pilgarlic,' volunteered Clara Garrity.

Kathy Sullivan asked, 'Is there going to be a raid tonight?'

'But what does it mean?' murmured Maureen Mulvaney. 'Have you any scones, Mary?'

The digestible quality of scones took conversational precedence, but Pilgarlic hung in the air like a smelly kipper.

Tom Kipper, Espionage Agent Extraordinaire, hidden behind the Shakespearean polished oak bookcase, smiled an enigmatic smile, for an idea had entered his Kipper head.

'Listen, Kinneally,' said Kipper, 'I have an idea.'

'What?' enquired Socks.

'I want you to help me tell a lie!'

'Wow,' said Kinneally for he had pronounced legions of lies, but had never been asked to invent one.

'When do we start and how much will you pay me?'

'Threepence.'

'Make it a tanner.'

'OK.'

'Let's start.'

'Now this is it and we have to write it neatly down.'

'You write – you're better than me.'

'Yes, but you tell better lies.'

With infinite racking of grey matter two masterminds steeped in mischief and guilt prepared a manuscript far exceeding any Greek tragedy written by W. Shakespeare.

It read:

'Garlic is a plant originating in Asia, probably Mongolia. It is made up of small segments called cloves which have a strong odour. When the Spanish Fleet, the Armada, was slashed to pieces by the brave British, led by Sir Francis Drake, many of their ships crashed on the Irish shore at McGillicuddy.

'The Irish, not being British, took the Spanish home to their huts and caves with lots of provisions from the Armada, including Garlic. The Irish planted them with their spuds but didn't tell the English. The Spaniards became known as the Black Irish.

'When English revenuers came knocking on the door

235

or knocking it down, the Black Irish would peel the skins off the garlic so that the poo-poo stink would drive the enemy to distraction, which it did.

'So "peeled-garlic" became a new word in the English language created by the Irish. Whenever mention was made of the English king, the cry would hit the rafters, "Oh, that bloody Peeled-Garlic!" which after several drops of the creature slipped into much usage as "Pilgarlic".

'Thus did the Irish colour the English Language.

'VERIFIED by the Royal Library of the United Kingdom LONDON 1926.'

'Smashing!' I hollered. 'Now let's go and see Betsy Braddock.'

Betsy Braddock was skipping rope in the quadrangle when we approached her. Her burnished red hair was tied tightly in pigtails secured by large pink bows. Her gingham dress was tied round her middle by a wide silk sash and the black lacquered shoes on her white stockinged feet shone with a polished gloss.

'What are you boys doing in the quad?' she enquired with haughty precision and brilliant eyes, for Betsy Braddock was quite superior, particularly to grubby boys.

'Listen, Braddy,' said Socks Kinneally, 'we want to know if you'll type something for us.'

She stopped skipping. 'Aren't you the boy who always tells lies? And don't call me Braddy!' She looked at him with great disdain as only Betsy Braddock can.

'I've never lied in me life,' lied Kinneally.

'Betsy, we need something typed,' I said. 'It's a piece of history and you're the only one with a typewriter to do it.'

She looked at me and almost smiled, for hidden in every Braddock heart is a reaching out to another, to everybody except Kinneally.

'You're Tom Kipper,' she smiled. 'My mother knows your mother.'

'Yes, me ma – I mean my mother – has mentioned Mrs Braddock. She said she makes the world's best mince pies. They go to meetings together.'

That was the clincher.

'Let me have a look.'

She took the paper, adjusted her wire-rimmed spectacles, read it faster than Uncle Bart's whippet, folded it and tucked it in her pocket.

'Friday is our very last day at school, so I'll give it to you tomorrow, Thomas,' she cooed, and recommenced skipping.

'He's not Thomas,' said Kinneally, 'he's Kipper.'

'Go away, horrible boy,' said Betsy Braddock. 'You are uncouth.'

'What does uncouth mean?' asked Kinneally.

Thus was almost born, a legend.

Nobody sailed on the ferry boats to Liverpool the following day because most of them were at the bottom of the Mersey in Davy Jones's Locker after Lord Haw-Haw verbally sent the glorious Luftwaffe over for several nights and our old red-bricked house on Woodstock Avenue was reduced to charcoal and spaghetti.

There was an ominous silence after that, except for shrapnel zinging down, dust falling in sheets. Which was when the cat, nicknamed Shrapnel, miaowed and brought us all to our senses.

The door to the wee shelter was hanging on its hinges after the Big One dropped. Thus I was able to put my big Scouser head through the open doorway and historically say, 'Look, Ma, no house!'

So we all helped Ma push the pram with the radio and the pussycat, Shrapnel, to a large empty house on a hill which had been vacated by its owners for the safer haven of Australia.

Thus did we take up residence on Mary Lane.

Two exhilarating days later, Socks Kinneally and I went to examine the interesting rubble at the old address.

High on a ledge at number thirty-seven Woodstock Avenue stood a super deluxe, leather bound, gold lettered library of Charles Dickens. It was enclosed in an elegant case in high relief, red leather, handsome books.

The geographic problem was to get your hands on them for the Luftwaffe had, with nasty intent, blown most of the charming house to pieces, leaving one corner of one upstairs bedroom serenely holding the Dickens bookcase. It almost looked dignified except for the utter chaos of ye olde English oak, red bricks and mortar littered as a backdrop.

'How are you going to get them down?' queried Socks Kinneally, staring upwards at Mount Dickens.

'Well,' I said, 'you see the wall on the left is like steps so I'll climb up them to the corner.'

'Then what?'

'Well, I'll throw them down to you one at a time. You used to be a good catcher.'

'The very best,' lied Socks.

I slipped once halfway up. Bits and pieces of number thirty-seven Woodstock Avenue cascaded down.

'You'll climb Mount Everest one day,' shouted Socks.

I leaned over at the summit to ease out a book – *The Pickwick Papers* – which I dropped to Kinneally, followed by *David Copperfield*, *Oliver Twist*, one by one the entire library, and then the case.

'I'm going to lever it like this,' I hollered, 'while you catch it.'

When Socks Kinneally picked himself up the bookcase was lying on the top with bricks underneath. 'You look like a sausage sandwich,' I ventured. 'Let's put in the books and carry the whole lot home.'

It was when I picked up *Great Expectations* that the letter fell out.

'What's that?' enquired Socks.

'It's an old letter, I think,' I said, 'and it has an Italian postage stamp on it.' I held it to the weak sunlight filtering through the ruins. 'I think it's addressed to me ma in her maiden name of Finnegan before she married me dad. It says Maria Finnegan. Me dad calls Ma "Maria" so it must be from him from Italy.'

'Hey, let's get these bloody books back to your place. Somebody left a wheelbarrow in the alley. Let's use that.'

'Isn't that stealing?'

'I hope so.'

At Mary Lane, Joseph Prendergast Kipper jumped with great joy at the return of his treasure, giving Socks Kinneally a shilling he took from Mum's purse. She gave Dad baleful glances later. But I kept the letter.

I looked at it over at Fossdike Park, on a bench under a sycamore tree by the side of the bowling green, for the bluish green ink on the envelope was faded by time. The print was like script.

There seemed to have been a wax seal, now faded, on the reverse side and I really felt in my heart of hearts that it was precious. Had it not been enclosed in *Great Expectations* these many sacred years, growing in that spirituality?

'I will not read it,' I said to myself in that park, on that bench, under that sycamore tree. The envelope had a faint hint of perfume mixed with age, that indefinable quality that has a bouquet, and the flap was open.

I found my fingers lifting the flap, revealing blue notepaper inside, one sheet it seemed, unlined, folded just once. 'Maria, Cara Mia,' it read, 'I am coming home to get you. That you will accept me as your husband is my "Great Expectation".' Then followed the message, then it ended, 'Maria, mi amore, ti amo. Arrivederci.'

Well, I did not read the message, not too much, anyway,

for I was trespassing into another world, but I was aware it was signed by 'Joseph' and it was dated October, 1918.

Tears came to my eyes for I remembered my dad had served with the British Forces in Italy in the 'War to End All Wars'. I wondered if Italian ice cream was as good as they said it was.

'Hey, la', watcha doin'?' shouted Socks Kinneally.

I got to my feet and put the letter away.

'I was just looking at that letter. Hey, you wanna go to Gregson's and pinch some apples?'

'Yeah!'

In the orchard Socks said, 'Your ma and a whole gang of other women are coming over to our place for tea and crumpets tonight.'

'And gossip.'

'What else.'

'You wonderful boy,' said Ma to Socks Kinneally when she saw the Charles Dickens bookcase after she returned from shopping at the village.

'What about me, Ma?'

'You're usually a Pilgarlic,' said my mother, 'but in this case you both get my special mince pies.'

No greater honour could be bestowed on any one human being, except the shilling Dad gave Socks.

'Why are you staring at me like that?' said Ma, who missed nothing with her Scotland Yard antennae. I mined into my gooey mince pie.

'I found something,' I said.

'What?' Blue Irish eyes bored into the depths of my soul, for Ma's Gaelic antennae took into chancery all messages of the wind.

For there exists in every man's being a spirit, not just the spirit of the soul, but a creation that inspires to matters abnormal, beyond the pale of Pilgarlic. It's like a great, golden cape thrown about your shoulders to guide you in times of adversity, hardship and humour. To the Irish heart, the Creator seems to have wrapped the great golden cape many times, so that in precious moments he walks with 'Himself'.

I took my ma by the hand – the hand that pounded scouse pots into oblivion, and led her into the living room, reached into the shelves of Charles Dickens and pulled out *Great Expectations*, placing it before her on the mahogany bureau, and turned pages to the middle to reveal two top secrets, one being the blessed epistle from Italy and the other 'The Defined History of Pilgarlic' which Socks and I had battered a thousand years or so to yellow parchment.

'*Great Expectations*, Ma,' I said.

She saw the letter immediately, clasped it to her bosom, tears on her cheeks. 'I thought I lost it forever,' she burbled.

As the tears subsided, she looked sharply at me.

'You didn't read it, did you?'

'Oh, no, Ma, it's private,' I lied, worse than Socks Kinneally.

'And what's this?'

'It was also in one of the books; I think it was inside *Sketches by Boz*.'

She unfolded the manuscript by Kipper and Kinneally, anonymous.

Clutching herself with one hand, her eyes lit up with splendid, overwhelming joy. 'Great merciful heavens, it's the glorious history of Pilgarlic! Oh, just wait till I read this tonight at Mrs Kinneally's house. I just can't wait!'

Who would have thought in this whole wide world that such a shard of vocal history could bring a cargo of revelatory joy to the heart, for it is written that in such wee things lie mountains of love and compassion.

'Is there any tea, Maria?' asked me dad from the depths of his Karl Marx armchair.

My mother, bless her, looked from the letter to Joseph Prendergast Kipper and said, smiling, 'Yes, there is.' And she kissed him on top of his greying thatch, which made him almost fall over.

And so I sneaked through the back door of the Kinneally residence that night to hide with Socks in shady recess until we saw Ma opening the yellowed manuscript to read the exposition of Pilgarlic to the great delight and gasps of the Mince Pie Gang.

She became a heroine, a Roman idol, a Greek goddess and an Irish saint all in one night.

'Absolutely smashing!' cried Aunt Madge.

'Glory be!' said Aunt Florence.

''Tis a complete revelation,' cried out Clara Garrity.

'Almost a miracle,' shouted Kathy Sullivan.

'All the saints be praised!' from Zilda Sweeney.

Maureen Mulvaney said, 'You're bloody crackers!'

Which is when Maureen Mulvaney became a Pilgarlic.

Socks and I smiled at each other.

'I feel guilty,' I said.

'So do I,' said Kinneally, which meant that he didn't.

It was then that the Mince Pie Gang discovered us hiding behind the sofa and we fled.

'That Tom Kipper,' said my mother, 'takes after his father. He's a real Pilgarlic! Friday is their last day at school. Only heaven knows his future.'

But then she smiled and when she did you could see the green, green fields of Ireland, the peat in the bog, the spud in the pot, the sparkle in the Guinness, the hidden charm of de Valera, the sauciness of Irish maidens, the bright eternal promise of it all, and very, very large mince pies.

And the verse was strumming gently in my mind as I brightly hummed 'Cara Mia mine, make my life divine'. Which is when I received a sharp slap behind the right ear.

'What was that for?' I indignantly enquired of my mother, Mary Catherine.

'You read it, didn't you?' she said.

'Aw gee, Ma!'

On Friday rain blew in from the North Sea, unexpectedly because the forecasters were chowing down on fish and chips and brown ale at the Dirty Duck. In one respect it was wonderful for it kept the Luftwaffe away and kept Merseyside its quite natural soggy self. Gutters ran like the

Mersey, raincoats glistened, spectacles streamed, feet became damp and the Academy of Hard Knocks overflowed with clientele.

The schoolyard was wet.

The last day in school didn't seem a great deal different from other days to me, for students were whacked with the same sticks; history was, of course, about the British Empire, which was crumbling in a dignified way like Grandpa's stack of kippers and Kinneally's New Year resolutions; history was about Normans invading, Henry VIII just having a most splendid time until his fifteen minutes of glory ran out. Sister Margaret Mary took Religious Class, smiling most times about the great glory to come.

'I wonder if they have ice cream with chocolate chip,' enquired Kinneally.

'An Irish mountain of it,' replied Sister Margaret Mary Coogan. The two classes leaving Hard Knocks assembled in the 'Great Hall' which was about the size of a large pot of good scouse, and 'Pop' Devereaux enlarged on the future, physically and spiritually, then they all cheered and ran like freed slaves from the Romans into the sunshine splitting the clouds over the Mersey.

It was a fight to get through the gate into Freedom Lane, past the Dirty Duck, the Bird in Hand, escapees from Hard Knocks.

'Hey, Kipper, let's go to County Park,' shouted Kinneally, dancing a Gaelic jig.

'I can't,' I lied, 'I have to do my job at the charming chandler on Reeds Lane.'

But I had a day off.

The sun was shining on Switchcross Lane as I trod softly and gently back the way I had come. The big iron gate was still open after discharging a fourteen-year-old mountain of tatty kids.

Not a soul stirred as I walked across the main playground by the grey and pink sandstone walls with the white wickets painted on them, at one of which Jimmy Laverty had creamed me with his bat. He had been avenged by Mrs O'Toole who creamed Laverty with her big brass bell.

Teaching staff had gone home too, cleaners had not yet arrived, Hard Knocks was going down to slumber.

I walked upright through the yards, past the church nave protruding into the junior play area, spiritual blocks of piety and foundation. At the corner of the gym I hoisted myself with fingers on a ledge to peer into Spiderlady McCann's torture chamber where her ghost was rapping knuckles with an outsize carpenter's rule.

'So, Tom Kipper,' the witch cackled, 'we have been misbehaving again!' Whack.

Shadows were lengthening across the quad.

'Boys,' said 'Pop', 'Devereaux your career now lies ahead of you; a great open space into which to invest yourselves. You could become investment councillors, priests, plumbers, policemen, executives. Now is the time to start your career.'

Career. Career. Career. The word fascinated my whole being, as I thought about Sean Maloney, Betsy Braddock,

Conks Murphy, Fred Magee, Maggie Donovan, Whacker Doyle, Gobs Flanagan, Sully.

But it was lonely in the Hard Knocks schoolyard. A great veil of silence enmeshed buildings and yards and I found myself with goose bumps, moisture at the corners of the blue Connemara eyes I had inherited from Mary Catherine Kipper.

An empty schoolyard, the loneliest place in the world.

As I trod towards the gate a shaft of sunlight streamed down on Hard Knocks and I found my step lighter as I entered the church, sunlight streaming rainbows through the leaded windows depicting the Holy Mother and a football gang of saints with the red lamp burning in a beaten copper compass.

'Thanks,' I said before stepping back into Switchcross Lane.

'Time for my career in Liverpool,' I found myself whispering as I broke into a run.

I wonder if Ma has any scouse in the pot . . .

Anything Goes

Billy Hopkins

It's December 1963 when Billy Hopkins and his wife Laura arrive home in Manchester after five years in Africa. The world has changed beyond recognition: now, it's the swinging sixties, with headlines full of the Beatles and the pill, LSD and mini skirts. Traditional values have been thrown into the melting pot.

Billy's youngest son still believes in Santa Claus and while his daughter's reading *Jackie*, she's not even a teenager yet, so Billy's not too worried about the impact of modern society on his family. He's more concerned about the welfare of his increasingly forgetful father and about the daily challenges he faces as a lecturer. When the four junior Hopkins start to choose their own, unexpected paths in life, though, Billy finds it harder than usual to see the funny side of things . . .

ANYTHING GOES brings readers close to a warm and loving family who somehow get through all their ups and downs without ever losing their sense of humour. Nostalgic, witty and at times sad, ANYTHING GOES is essential reading for everyone who has ever been a parent, or ever rebelled against their own.

Billy Hopkins' novels have been warmly acclaimed:

'How wonderful to have a book like this . . . that pulls the reader back to that different world' *Manchester Evening News*

'Filled with humour and warmth . . . the compelling story of one family's journey to a land of dreams, challenges and heartache' *Knutsford Guardian*

'Not only is it a heart-rending story, it is a remarkable piece of social history' *Lancashire Magazine*

978 0 7553 2055 4

headline

DON'T WAKE ME AT DOYLES

MAURA MURPHY

'I woke up and saw myself as a human being again. For the first time in my life I had something to say. My mind came alive with the memories of my childhood. Words began to flow . . . No more would I be the "illiterate fool" that John called me'

When seventy-five-year-old Maura Murphy discovered she had cancer, she left her husband of fifty years and started recording her story. Fearlessly honest, Maura's memoir takes you from her early days running wild in the 1920s Irish countryside, to her destructive marriage to a hard-working, hard-drinking womaniser, the birth of her nine children, leaving Ireland for 1950s Birmingham, and a life-or-death choice that would change her for ever.

Told with biting wit, *Don't Wake me at Doyles* contains all the explosive power of *Angela's Ashes* – a remarkable story of an ordinary woman and an extraordinary life.

NON-FICTION / MEMOIR 978 0 7553 1305 1

Now you can buy any of these other bestselling Headline books by from your bookshop or *direct from the publisher*.

FREE P&P AND UK DELIVERY
(Overseas and Ireland £3.50 per book)

Anything Goes	Billy Hopkins	£6.99
As Time Goes By	Harry Bowling	£6.99
You Stole My Heart Away	Joan Jonker	£6.99
The Other Side of the Track	Victor Pemberton	£5.99
Don't Wake Me at Doyles	Maura Murphy	£7.99

TO ORDER SIMPLY CALL THIS NUMBER

01235 400 414

or visit our website: www.madaboutbooks.com

Prices and availability subject to change without notice.